Duncan watched as Lauren turned those incredible eyes on him

"So, you're a pool shark, huh? And you accused me of being one."

He was glad that he hadn't been able to sleep tonight, that he'd gone out to get a drink because his room had seemed so vast and empty. He liked being here with her. "I'm not that good. Trust me."

She smiled at him, a gentle expression, and he wished he could make her smile on command. "We'll see, won't we?"

He found himself staring at her lips, and looked away. Needing a distraction—fast—he took his shot. A striped ball fell into the corner pocket, another one dropped into a side pocket.

They continued to play, and he was doing well until he sensed Lauren behind him and missed.

"Too bad," she murmured as she leaned halfway across the table, lined up her shot, called it and made it. Along with two more. He studied the table, and couldn't take his eyes off her.

Duncan wanted to get to know her. He wanted to know what made Lauren Carter tick.

And he had some pretty good ideas about how he'd go about finding that out.

Dear Reader,

Discovering Duncan is the first of four books in my RETURN TO SILVER CREEK series.

Lauren Carter goes to Silver Creek, a small skiing town in the high mountain country of Nevada, as a private investigator. She's trying to track down Duncan Bishop, a man who has all but dropped out of his world. She expects to find a man running away, a man who has turned his back on his wealth and power, but instead she finds a man in search of himself, a man going back to his past to find his future.

Returning to Silver Creek lets four men who are at life-changing moments discover that they can indeed go home again. And that sometimes the answers are where we least expect to find them.

I hope you enjoy *Discovering Duncan*, and will look for my next book, *Judging Joshua*, in August 2005.

DISCOVERING DUNCAN
Mary Anne Wilson

TORONTO • NEW YORK • LONDON
AMSTERDAM • PARIS • SYDNEY • HAMBURG
STOCKHOLM • ATHENS • TOKYO • MILAN • MADRID
PRAGUE • WARSAW • BUDAPEST • AUCKLAND

ISBN 0-373-75066-8

DISCOVERING DUNCAN

www.eHarlequin.com

Printed in U.S.A.

ABOUT THE AUTHOR

Mary Anne Wilson is a Canadian transplanted to Southern California, where she lives with her husband, three children and an assortment of animals. She knew she wanted to write romances when she found herself "rewriting" the great stories in literature, such as *A Tale of Two Cities*, to give them "happy endings." Over her long career she's published more than thirty romances, had her books on bestseller lists, been nominated for Reviewer's Choice Awards and received a Career Achievement Award in Romantic Suspense. She's looking forward to her next thirty books.

Books by Mary Anne Wilson

HARLEQUIN AMERICAN ROMANCE

*Just for Kids
†Return to Silver Creek

For Taylor Anne Levin.
I love you more than you can say you love me!

Chapter One

"It's nothing personal. This is business."

Duncan Bishop stared down at his father who sat behind the huge wood-and-marble desk in the private office of the CEO of Bishop International. The room was dead silent as the old man's words faded into nothingness.

Duncan Ross Bishop, or D.R. as he liked to be called, stared right back at his son, a look on his face that Duncan had seen many times in the years he'd been part of the Bishop business dealings. The "I'm doing it my way, so get out of my way" look. Before it had been annoying, maybe even frustrating, but now it was sickening.

"Gary Tellgare is a friend."

D. R. Bishop, a giant of a man, was as fit and hard physically as he was in the business world. With a full head of snow-white hair, a neatly trimmed beard to match, a deeply tanned complexion and a penchant for dark suits that emphasized his size, he knew how to intimidate. With the wave of a hand, he lopped off heads in business and never flinched.

Now he waved his large hand dismissively at Duncan on the other side of the desk. "Damn it, that doesn't have any bearing on this. There are no friends in business. We need his routing division, and Tellgare runs a half-baked company that doesn't need it. So, we get it…any way we can."

Although Duncan never wore a beard, and his hair was dark brown with gold highlights, he matched his father physically with a solid, six-foot-three-inch frame, tanned skin, dark brown eyes and a penchant for dark, three-piece business suits. But other than DNA, right now they had nothing in common. "You've crossed the line if you try to ruin Tellgare."

D.R. rocked his leather chair back, tented his fingers and studied his son with eyes as dark as night. "Crossed the line?"

Duncan leaned forward, pressing both palms down on the reflective surface of the cold desk. "Damn straight."

"Oh, come on," D.R. said with an exaggerated sigh. "I don't have time for this bleeding-heart garbage. Just get it done."

Duncan had heard those words before, and he was incredibly tired of them. He felt numb from watching his father destroy anything in his path. "I don't have time for this, either," he finally said as he straightened.

"Then get on with it." D.R. pushed a folder on his desk over to Duncan. "Get to Legal and tell them to change this."

He ignored the file. "No. If you're going after Tellgare, count me out."

The folder sat between them as D.R. drilled Duncan with a ferocious glare. "What?" he demanded.

"Are you going after Tellgare?"

"To use your words, damn straight." The older man sat back and crossed his arms on his chest. "*Damn* straight."

Dark eyes held dark eyes without blinking. For one week, Duncan had known this move was coming. He'd known there was no hope of stopping D.R. this time. "Unless you let me take over now and you step down, I'm out of here."

D.R. uttered a profanity that rocked the room around them. "Fat chance of me stepping down and handing you all of this."

"It's your company and your decision. Live with both of them," Duncan said. "I've had it."

"You've had it?" D.R. stood to his full size. "News flash, Duncan, so have I. I've put up with your arguments and your flawed reasoning more than I should have because you're my son. But no more. It's my company, and I'll do things my way. So get over it, and get on with this business with Tellgare."

Now that he'd made the decision to quit, Duncan was shocked he had no second thoughts. "That's it?"

D.R. exhaled. "And I quote, 'Damn straight.'"

Duncan turned for the door, but D.R. wasn't finished.

"Don't you walk out on me like this!" the man thundered.

Duncan reached for the brass door handle.

"Don't you think you're going to use anything I

taught you to go up against this company," D.R. said, enraged. "If you walk out the door, you're dead in this town. You're done."

Duncan twisted the cold handle.

"What in the hell do you think Adrianna is going to say about this idiocy?" D.R. demanded.

Duncan stopped, but didn't turn. Adrianna? Tall, blond and no stranger to the business world, Adrianna Barr was the only child of one of the most powerful bankers on the West Coast. They'd dated, had fun, and they understood each other. "She'll understand."

D.R.'s boom of laughter filled the office. "God, you're deluded. She'll drop you like a bad habit."

Maybe D.R. was right, and maybe he was wrong. It didn't matter right then. Maybe it would later, but not then. Duncan was used to being alone. He'd always been alone. "Whatever." Duncan jerked the door open.

"Where are you going?" his father asked, closer now, almost behind him.

Duncan turned and stood eye to eye, toe to toe with his father. "Anywhere but here."

D.R. exhaled, raking his fingers through his thick white hair, then waved a hand vaguely. "Oh, just go home, get drunk, get Adrianna and take a break. I can handle things on this end."

"And Tellgare?" he asked in a low voice.

"Leave it to me. I'll do it if you don't have the stomach for it." There was no backing down when it came to his father. None at all. There never had been. "Branch or Gills can take over for you this time."

D.R. still didn't get it. "There won't be a next time."

D.R. flushed red and he rocked forward on the balls of his feet, bringing his face inches from his son's. "Listen to me. You're a Bishop, born and bred. You *are* my son, and the only Bishop left once I'm gone. Walking out won't change that."

Duncan shook his head. "No, nothing can change that, but I'll learn to live with it."

Then he turned and walked away. D.R. yelled from the door of his private office, but not at Duncan. He yelled at his secretary, a middle-aged woman who had been with D.R. for ten years. "Helen, call security. Mr. Bishop is leaving. He's to take nothing with him, have no access to his office or anything to do with this company."

Helen chanced a furtive glance at Duncan, and he could see the look of commiseration on her face. She knew what it was like to be browbeaten by the CEO. As he strode out the main office door, the last thing he heard was Helen saying, "Yes, sir, right away, sir."

Duncan didn't go anywhere near his office. He went straight down to the parking garage, got in his car and took nothing with him when he went through the security gates for the last time. He didn't look back as he pulled out onto the congested streets of downtown Los Angeles bathed in the late afternoon sun of a clear May day. He drove to his apartment, packed his bags, told the superintendent he'd be in contact and left.

When he met with Adrianna, he found out the old man had been right about at least one thing. Adrianna wasn't having any part of his explanations. She didn't get it, either. Finally, he gave up and left her, too. When he drove away from Los Angeles, he drove away from his old life and everything in it. And he didn't look back.

Los Angeles,
Six Months Later:

"I'M A MAN OF PATIENCE," D. R. Bishop said as his secretary left, closing the door securely behind her. "But even I have my limits."

Lauren Carter never took her eyes off the large man across the impressive wood-and-marble desk. D. R. Bishop was dressed all in black. He was a huge, imposing man, and definitely, despite what he said, a man with little patience. He looked tightly wound and ready to spring.

Lauren sat very still in a terribly uncomfortable chair, her hands in her lap while she let D. R. Bishop do all the talking. She simply nodded from time to time. The longer he talked, she got the impression he was the type who drove his life by the sheer force of his will, the same way he did business.

"My son walked out on everything six months ago," he said.

She finally spoke. "Why?"

He tented his fingers thoughtfully with his elbows resting on the polished desktop as if he were considering her single-word question. But she knew he was considering just how much to tell her. His eyes were dark as night, a contrast to his snow-white hair and meticulously trimmed beard. "Ah, that's a good question," he said, hedging for some reason.

"Mr. Bishop, you've dealt with the Sutton Agency enough to know that privacy and discretion are part and parcel of our service. Nothing you tell me will go any further."

He shrugged his massive shoulders and sank back in his chair. "Of course. I expect no less," he said.

"Why did your son leave?"

"I thought it was a middle-age crisis of some sort." He smiled slightly, a strained expression. "Not that thirty-eight is middle aged. Then I thought he might be having a breakdown. Maybe gone over the edge." The man stood abruptly, rising to his full, imposing height, and she could have sworn she felt the air ripple around her from his movement. "But he's not crazy, Ms. Carter, he's just damn stubborn. Too damn stubborn."

She waited as he walked to the windows behind him and faced the city twenty floors below. When he didn't speak again, she finally said, "You don't know why he left?"

The shoulders shrugged again sharply. "A difference of opinion on how to do business. Nothing new for us." He spoke without turning. "We've always clashed, but in the end, we've always managed to make our business relationship work."

The two of them had made Bishop International a force to be reckoned with in the financial world. When he didn't speak again for several minutes, she knew she wasn't going to get more on the "whys" of his son leaving. Even though she'd been working as a private investigator for less than a year, Lauren knew when she was hitting a concrete wall, when the client wasn't about to disclose personal information.

She took a notebook and pen out of her purse and got to the point of the meeting. "What do you want from the Sutton Agency exactly, Mr. Bishop?"

"Find him."

"That's it?"

He turned back to her, studying her intently for several moments before he said, "No."

"Then what else do you want us to do?"

"As an employee of Sutton, I want you to find my son, and I want him to come back here, willingly."

"Okay," she said.

He gripped the back of his chair, pressing his long fingers into the plush leather. "I'm going to offer you something that's just between the two of us, and no one else. Agreed?"

"I don't know what you're talking about, so I can hardly agree to it."

He let go of the chair and came around to where she was and sat on the edge of his desk. She had no doubt every move he made was well thought out for maximum effect on the person he was facing. She was tall for a woman at five-nine, but still shorter than he was by half a foot, and he outweighed her hundred and twenty-five pounds by a lot. Now he was looking down at her intently, and it was all she could do to stay seated and not stand to minimize his advantage.

"He's a barracuda." That's what Vern Sutton, her boss at the Sutton Agency, had told her when she'd been assigned to this job. "The man is tough as nails and gets what he wants. He doesn't care how he does it, either." The agency had done a number of background checks for D. R. Bishop over the years, on employees, business associates and even personal acquaintances. But they had never handled a missing person's case for them.

D.R. had personally called the agency this time, said he needed to locate a missing person, and he'd asked for her specifically to be on the case. He hadn't given Vern a reason, and Vern hadn't asked. He also hadn't told Vern the missing person was his own son.

"Why don't you just explain things to me, and then I can make a decision? No matter how this turns out, it will be kept confidential," she finally said when she couldn't stand the silence between them any longer. "But I can't make any decision until I know what's involved."

"That sounds doable," he said. "I want you to find Duncan. See where he's gone, and what he's doing. Meet him, interact with him and figure out a way to get him back here of his own accord. Then we'll have a deal between the two of us, an incentive if you'd like."

She wasn't going to play a guessing game with him. "Why don't you just tell me what you're talking about?"

He nodded faintly as if she'd passed some test. "If you can get my son to come back here willingly, I'll of course pay the agency's bill, but I'll make another payment that will go directly to you. A bonus. From me, to you."

"Just for getting him back here?"

"Yes, and how you do it is up to you. Just do it."

"And the payment?" she asked, cutting to the chase.

He named a figure that was not only outrageous, but, incredibly, it was the sum total of the tuition payments she'd need to finish law school, almost to the penny. She simply sat and stared at D. R. Bishop as she realized that he'd obviously had *her* investigated before he ever approached Vern about her services. He knew what she needed and why she was working at the agency. He'd looked over the operatives and found the most needy one.

"So, could you use the money?" he asked evenly.

She wanted to say, "You know I can," but settled for, "Of course, who couldn't?"

"Then it's yours, if you deliver."

"Mr. Bishop, what happens if your son won't come back?"

The older man actually frowned, as though he'd never considered that option. "Then I pay your boss and you get your usual cut. End of deal," he said abruptly.

God, she hated people like him. People who had to be in control, who had to have power, and people who wielded that power as easily as they breathed. His son was probably the mirror image of the man, brought up in his likeness. Duncan Bishop had probably walked out because they couldn't agree on how to destroy someone or something. Knife, gun or poison. She just bet the father chose a knife so he could destroy "up close and personal," while the son wanted the gun to get things over with quickly.

She finally stood to face him. "Just get him to come back to L.A.?"

"He comes back and you can get your law degree."

He didn't care that she knew he'd had her investigated. "That's an interesting offer," she said.

"If you do this successfully, maybe when you pass the California bar exam, there'll be a place for you around here."

She didn't try to stop the smile that came at his words. He'd obviously just looked into her financial needs and didn't know what she was going to law school for. "That sounds enticing, sir, and I appreciate the thought, but I'm going to specialize in criminal law."

The old man burst into a guffaw of laughter. "Damn, maybe we could use you anyway," he said.

"You never know," she murmured.

He turned from her to go around and drop back down onto his leather chair. He reached for a box that had been on the desk since she arrived. "Here's everything you'll need to know about Duncan. His connections, relationships, interests, his business background, pictures."

"How about credit cards?"

"Helen made a list for you and it's in there."

"Money?"

"I don't know what he took, but he has access through his accounts. Helen put that information in there, too."

"Has he made any business connections since he left?"

"No."

"Where did he live when he was in L.A.?"

"He was in the Edge Water Towers off of Wilshire."

A moneyed area. "Owned or rented?"

"Owned, but he leased it out when he left for a year."

"Through whom?"

"The agent who deals with those units." He gave her the name, and she wrote it down in her notebook.

"Did he live there alone?"

"When he wanted to. But he's seldom wanted to." His eyes narrowed. "Ms. Carter, my son likes women. He's seldom without a woman, and if he is, it's his choice." He deliberately let his eyes flicker over her, then back to meet her gaze. "As I said, do anything you need to do to get his attention and get him back here." He smiled slightly and it had the power to unnerve her. "Do we understand each other?"

She understood and it made her vaguely sick. No wonder he'd asked for a woman. The man thought that seduction was all part of the package. It wasn't. "Of course," she said. "I understand. Is he married, divorced, involved?"

"No, no and no. He had a girlfriend, Adrianna Barr, but that's a thing of the past. She took a walk when he did."

She'd heard of the woman, a society brat from all that she'd read about her, the daughter of a wealthy banker. She'd even seen pictures of the socialite out and about at society parties. Very blond, very pretty, very pale, very thin and very rich. And he thought she, Lauren, could seduce his son into coming back here? Wrong again.

She wasn't any Adrianna Barr. If D. R. Bishop had bothered to really look at her, he'd see that even though she was tall enough, she wasn't pale, she wasn't skinny and she didn't have long blond hair. And she sure as heck wasn't rich.

Lauren was tanned, always was, winter or summer, with a generous amount of freckles. She had curves that refused to give her that popular boyish look in stylish clothes, and her hair was deep auburn, bordering on red, cut short and feathered around her face. On top of that, she had no society connections and her bank balance was laughable.

"Okay," she murmured, making a show of writing something in her notebook. He wouldn't know she was writing "Fat chance" in cursive, then underlining it. She closed the book and looked back at the man, barely able to hide her distaste. But she managed to. "Anything else you can think of?"

"No," D.R. said as he held the box out to her.

She pushed her notebook into her purse, then put the strap over her shoulder and took the box, a bit surprised at how heavy it was. "Is there any family he'd go visit?"

D.R. shook his head. "None. He's an only child and his mother's been gone ten years."

She held the box to her middle. "Any gut feelings about where he'd go, what he'd do?"

He shook his head again. "No."

"In the entire six months there's been no contact?"

"Not directly."

"What does that mean?"

He motioned to the box. "It's all in there. My people found him in Dallas and he took off."

"They can't find him again?"

"They could, but he'd just leave again. That's why I need you. He won't know a thing, until you work your magic." He smiled at her, as if to ingratiate himself with her. "And my instincts tell me you can do it."

She made herself nod and say, "I'll do my best," then ask, "How do you want the updates? Daily, weekly…?"

"Once."

"Excuse me?"

"Just call me when he's on his way home."

"That's it?"

"Unless you blow it, then file your report, let your boss bill me and that's that."

She paused. "Sir, one more thing?"

"Of course."

"He ran away, like some teenager. I don't get it."

"He didn't. He left. He cut off everything, and he left. He told me he'd never be back, and I won't accept that. This is where he belongs. He's my only heir, the person who takes over when I'm gone. I need him back here."

She had the feeling that his last sentence was his most truthful. He needed his son back with him. Not only for professional reasons but because he missed him. "Okay, Mr. Bishop," she said. "I'll be in touch."

She carried the box down to the parking garage level and got into her car, an unmemorable blue compact. She put the box on the passenger seat, opened it and reached for the papers on top—newspaper clippings, a copy of a birth certificate, several photos.

Duncan Bishop was the spitting image of his father, only younger. He had the intense dark eyes. Every photo of the man had him looking right into the camera, as if he met the world head on and didn't flinch. His features weren't perfect, but the strong jaw and high cheekbones combined to make the man "interesting." His hair was short enough, styled back from his face, a dark brown shot with gold highlights, and every photo had him in a business suit or tuxedo. In one picture she found the Barr woman with him, his arm around her, the woman smiling at someone nearby, the man looking at the camera, appearing faintly bored.

She sorted through, got to the newspaper clippings and wasn't surprised to see they were all about the business, all about the father and son making a deadly team. All about the victories of the Bishops. She put them back in the box, then looked at the birth certificate. Duncan Ross Bishop. Son of Ellen Gayle O'Hara and Duncan Ross Bishop. His birthday was a month away, two weeks before Christmas. She glanced at the birthplace. Silver Creek, Nevada. She'd heard of the place, but only because of a posh ski resort located there, a very expensive, very in-demand and very private place. A place a Bishop could afford, and, coincidentally, Duncan Bishop's home.

A lot of people went home when they "disappeared," and she wondered if Duncan Bishop was that predictable. Would she find him at the fancy resort there, The Inn at Silver Creek? Maybe he was there partying. Or hiding.

Whatever the case, she'd find him. Her future depended on it.

Chapter Two

Lauren found Duncan Bishop in one week, and if there hadn't been a weekend plunked down in there, she would have found him faster. She looked for hits on his credit cards, his social security card and bank withdrawals. The hits had been all over the country on a personal credit card that wasn't associated with the company. She'd followed the pattern, and that pattern had ended up where she'd first thought to look—Silver Creek, Nevada. It had been almost too easy.

One week after she'd met with D. R. Bishop, she was picking up a rental car in Las Vegas, carrying no luggage and with a return flight to Los Angeles that night at ten o'clock. She drove north through the expansive desert, and finally climbed into the Sierra Nevada Mountains, heading up into rugged country. The one thing she hadn't discovered was where in Silver Creek he was. He wasn't at The Inn at Silver Creek north of the town. He wasn't holed up in an obscenely expensive grouping of cottages that the rich and sometimes famous rented. He wasn't sitting around a roaring fire in the evenings sipping cognac and rubbing shoulders with people like him. But he was in Silver Creek.

She'd found one place where the credit charges repeated themselves, a place called Rusty's Diner. She found out that the diner was in the oldest section of town, the part that had survived from the early days when Silver Creek had been part of the huge silver-mining industry in the area. Rusty's was owned by Dwayne Altman, sixty-five, with a bank balance that showed the diner did okay, but wasn't in the same league as the trendy restaurants and cafés in the newer section of town.

She had no idea what Duncan Bishop was doing at Rusty's, but when she had called the place and asked for him, the woman who answered had said, "He's not in right now. Want to leave a message?" Lauren had hung up. She hadn't been able to find anything in the records of the town with Duncan's name on it, so she had to assume that he was either a customer who came in so regularly that they took calls for him there, or he worked there. Neither made sense to her. So she headed to Silver Creek to find Duncan Bishop, figure out what he was doing there and form a plan of action.

By the middle of the afternoon, she'd made it to Silver Creek, found Rusty's Diner and was sitting across from it at a coffee shop with benches and tables outside on the wooden walkway that lined both sides of the street. She held an untouched cup of coffee, and waited. The diner across the street was rustic, but not in a fake way. It really was old, the wooden siding on it worn from time and weather, and the sign looked as if it had been there since the silver-mining days.

She glanced around at an area that was typical of any old mining town. It fanned out from the main street, a narrow two-lane thoroughfare, lined by brick and wooden buildings, its growth limited by the soaring mountains on either side of the pass. She could see skiing shops, antique stores, a museum to the north, a few bars, even some houses squeezed in here and there. Rusty's sat between an art gallery that advertised "Silver Creek Primitive Art," and a postal shipping center.

She glanced back at the coffee shop where she sat, and saw a brass plaque by the door declaring it had once been "the assay office for this whole territory." Now it was a place that served "over 100 specialty coffees." She sipped some of her own coffee, glanced across the street and saw the front door to the diner open. A large man in rough outdoor clothes—from a heavy navy jacket to worn Levi's, heavy boots and a dark watch cap pulled low—stepped outside.

He was the right size, but she couldn't get a good look at his face. So she watched him cross the wooden walkway, go to his right, and for a minute she was sure he was heading down the street. If he'd taken off, she would have followed, just in case she'd found Duncan Bishop.

Then luck was with her. He stopped at a large, new SUV, with Nevada dealer plates still on it. As he reached for the handle on the back cargo door, he paused and looked up, almost looking right at her. But his gaze swept past her, down the walkway to her right. He watched as a group of rowdy kids in expensive ski clothes came down the walkway. They stopped at a souvenir shop two doors down from where she sat, then the man went back to opening the door.

She sighed with relief because he hadn't been looking at her, and because, with one glimpse of his face in the late afternoon sun, she knew she'd found Duncan Bishop. But he wasn't the Duncan Bishop she'd seen in the pictures and clippings. This man looked like a rugged, blue-collar worker. He moved quickly, took two heavy boxes out of the new SUV, closed the door and headed back to the diner. She stayed where she was, waiting, but Duncan Bishop didn't come back out.

She sipped a bit more of her now tepid coffee, then stood, tossing the paper coffee cup in a trash can by the table, then pushed her hands in the pockets of her plain navy jacket. Nothing about her stood out, except maybe her hair color and she hadn't had time to do anything about that. So she opted for a knit ski cap she'd found in a supply store near where she'd parked the rental car. She had tugged it as low as she could to cover as much of her hair as possible.

Lauren hunched her shoulders into the cold, biting wind that seemed to have come from nowhere as she stepped down off the walkway and onto the parking shoulder. She waited for a car to pass, then she hurried across to Rusty's. She pushed back the entry door and stepped inside. The diner was larger than it looked from the street, and was decorated in wood and stone.

Booths lined the front wall, and tables were covered with red-checkered tablecloths that surrounded a huge stone fireplace framed by more booths along the side wall. A bar was against the back wall, with the kitchen visible through an order window. The air was warm and smelled wonderful from a mixture of coffee and cinnamon. Soft music played in the background, Christmas music that was over a month early. As she stood absorbing the atmosphere, a waitress spotted her.

The thin, blond woman in jeans and a red-checkered shirt strode over to her in the entry and smiled. "Welcome, welcome." She motioned to the almost empty restaurant. "Take your choice."

"Thanks," she said and moved to a booth by the front wall, where she could observe the whole layout without looking obvious.

She sank onto the plastic seat, took the menu the waitress offered and asked for a glass of water. When the waitress left, she picked up the menu, ready to use it as a prop so she could look over its edge. But she'd barely opened it when a man came out of a side hall off the entry. She had a pretty good idea who he was—Dwayne Altman, the owner.

He was the right age, medium height, a bit of a paunch under a gray-flannel shirt he wore with Levi's, and his hair and full beard were a deep red. He spoke to the waitress and then made his way to the kitchen.

As Lauren watched him through the order window, the waitress returned to her table, and Lauren ordered a grilled-cheese sandwich to go and a cup of tea while she waited. As the woman headed back to put in the order, Lauren sat back in the booth and casually studied the rest of the room. Paneled walls, heavy beams overhead, rustic chandeliers that looked as if they were made of antlers and a huge deer head over the stone fireplace.

She looked away from the trophy and glanced at the entry. A four-shelf unit on the wall by the cash register held an assortment of mugs, all different and all carefully arranged. Above the shelves was a wood carved sign, Home Is Where You Hang Your Mug.

She glanced back at the kitchen, but the only person she could see through the half window was the cook. Not Duncan Bishop. She was beginning to think he'd ducked out another door she hadn't been able to see from her vantage point. Then she saw him come out of the side hall. He was headed for the kitchen.

His watch cap was off, his jacket undone and he walked quickly, with long strides. He stepped into the kitchen, and as the door swung shut, the waitress appeared with her tea. She took it, but never drank it. She watched as Rusty and Duncan came out of the kitchen and walked toward the front of the diner.

They stopped at the greeting desk, with Rusty's back to her and Duncan facing the restaurant. He looked up and his gaze met hers for a fraction of a second before turning away and refocusing on Rusty. She quickly looked down into her cup of steaming tea, but listened intently to their conversation.

"Hey, it sounds good to me and I appreciate you doing it," Rusty was saying. "I wouldn't know where to start dealing like that."

"Okay." Lauren glanced up from her tea at the sound of Duncan Bishop's voice. It was deep like his father's, a bit more rough, and carried easily in the almost empty restaurant. He was tugging at the sleeves of his jacket as he talked to the other man. "I'll be back here no later than five p.m. on Thursday."

"You watch yourself driving on that highway," Rusty said. "And watch your back in Vegas."

"I intend to," Duncan said as he pulled his watch cap out of his pocket and put it on. Then he left. Through the windows, Lauren saw him stride across to the new SUV he'd gone to earlier.

He was leaving, going to Las Vegas, and she couldn't follow him. She couldn't get outside fast enough to get to her car and trail him. And she didn't think, even if she could, that it would be a good idea. She didn't know where he was going, but she knew he'd be back here on Thursday by five. Three days, days she could use to figure out how to approach him, how to get close enough to find out more about him and, in the end, get him to go back where he belonged.

She watched him stop just as he was about to go around the front of the SUV, turn and look back up the street. She twisted to see what he was looking at and saw the same kids who had made a commotion earlier. A gang of kids with time on their hands and money enough to get into trouble.

Three of them broke away from the main group of six or seven, and caught up with a girl who was probably in her late teens, very tiny and pretty, in a bright pink skiing outfit. The three were yelling at her, laughing uproariously, catching up quickly. She was obviously trying to ignore them, but she didn't make it past Rusty's before they were on her, circling her like a pack of hyenas right near Duncan and the SUV.

One of the guys, wearing loose, hanging pants, ski boots and a bulky down jacket, made a grab for her arm to stop her. He caught her by the sleeve, pulling her back and spinning her around. Even through the glass, Lauren heard her say, "Just let go of me, you creep!"

The other two were laughing, blocking her way if she tried to keep going. Then things changed. The one who had a hold on the girl moved backward, but not of his own volition. Duncan was there with a handful of the guy's jacket, pulling him away from the girl as if he weighed nothing. The kid turned, his hand balled into a fist, then reconsidered doing something drastic when he found himself facing Duncan, who was a good eight inches taller than him. He twisted, and Duncan let him go, and when one of the other two started to say something, he hushed his friend with a slap on the kid's upper arm.

Duncan was talking, his voice so low she couldn't hear it at all, but the boys heard it. Duncan's expression was unreadable, giving away nothing. Not anger, not disgust, or even aggression, but Lauren waited for something to explode. It never did.

Instead, Duncan was leaning toward the ring leader, using his size the way his father did. He got close, and all three of the hoodlums backed up, shook their heads in unison and, quite remarkably, walked away…quickly, without looking back once. The girl was watching them with wide eyes, then looked up at Duncan, touched his arm. Lauren could see her cheeks were flushed as she spoke to him.

Duncan shook his head as he said something to her, then, with a nod, he went back to his SUV. But he didn't get in. He went around it and kept walking across the street, to the far side, and disappeared from sight. Dusk was approaching. Old-fashioned lamps lined the street and flashed to life. Twinkling Christmas lights framed display windows and outlined rooflines.

"Here you go," someone said, and Lauren looked up at the waitress who was putting a take-out container on the table. "Anything else for you tonight?"

"No, no thanks," she said.

"Thanks for coming in," the waitress said, laying the bill on top of the take-out carton. Lauren paid and left. Stepping out into the chilly twilight, she hurried down the street to her rental car. Once she got the heat going she sat and ate the sandwich.

Duncan Bishop had walked off without his car. One of the charges on his personal credit card had been for Silver Creek Hotel. She'd looked it up, expecting to find a luxury hotel, but she'd been wrong. It was the original hotel in the town, built back in the 1800s, with only twenty rooms in all, and the charges had been recurring, every two weeks. From the address, she'd mapped it as two blocks north of Rusty's. If he was on foot, chances were, he'd gone there. She wouldn't attempt to watch him again. Not tonight.

She looked up the street to the north, where more lights were flashing to life. Ski slopes were defined by climbing brilliance on the west, some close and some a lot farther away. As the heat built to a comfortable level in the car, she mulled over everything she'd seen, heard and found out today. Nibbling on her sandwich, she let the facts settle and she gradually formulated a plan.

She started humming "Jingle Bells" under her breath as she pushed the napkins into the carryout box, then put the car in gear and tipped the vents so the warm air touched her face. She had the ten o'clock return flight, but she wasn't going to make it. She had to see a few more things, then she could head back to Las Vegas. She got on the cell phone, had enough signal to get her call through and pushed her flight reservation back to midnight. Then she drove away from the curb and headed north.

She spotted the hotel on the left as she drove. It was a three-story brick building, with a steeply pitched roof. Tall, narrow windows lined the walls downstairs, and broader windows overlooked the street from the second floor. There was a parking area to the right, and white twinkling lights framed the entry with its half-wood and half-glass door. A sign was hung above the door: The Silver Creek Hotel, Est. 1858. Another sign in a front window seemed jarringly modern and announced Vacancies.

She kept driving, out of the older part of town, into a newer, more developed area. She passed a cluster of restaurants, then the public ski lifts. There was snow on the slopes, but nowhere else. The talk at the coffee shop had been complaints about no snow, how late the season was and how unsatisfactory it was skiing on machine-made snow. The shops at the foot of the lifts were closed, as well.

She kept driving up the street lined with small cabins and homes, and headed into a more upscale area.

Here, the shops were high end, the restaurants fancy, and estates were hidden behind massive security gates and high fences. She could see some homes built up the mountains, their lights cutting through the growing darkness.

She turned to follow a bend in the road and the lights from the ski slopes were glowing into the night sky. She saw what she thought was a street to her left, with soft pillar lights framing it, and a wide, sweeping turnoff. But as she got closer, she could see it was an elaborate security entrance.

The pavement was made of cobbled stones, leading up to a lit gatehouse with a security guard standing by, watching the road. Behind him were six-foot-high carved wooden gates hung on massive stone pillars. Carriage lights lit the way and showed just a portion of the stone wall that ran off to the right and left. A rock arch swept over the top of the gates and, illuminated by hidden lights, brass letters spelled out The Inn at Silver Creek.

The place was completely blocked by gates, fences and the guard who looked in her direction when he heard her car approaching. When he saw she was in a cheap import, he lost interest and went back to looking at a pad of paper he had in his hand. Lauren drove a bit farther, never finding the end of the high stone fence, and never finding any life outside of it, either. She finally turned and retraced her route. When she got to the resort's entry it was dark, and she watched as a low black sports car cut in front of her to get to the gates.

She slowed, watching the guard walk up to the driver's window, glance inside, then wave the car through.

The gates opened slowly, and for a moment Lauren could see beyond the barriers. She caught a glimpse of a lit road heading into the compound, going toward a series of sprawling buildings. Beyond, ski slopes glowed in the darkness.

She didn't have any idea why Duncan Bishop was holed up at the Silver Creek Hotel, and not here. But she'd find out. She drove on until she was at the hotel and saw the phone number under the vacancy sign. She memorized it, then pulled into a parking spot a few buildings down and took out her cell phone. It only had one bar of signal, but she punched in the number and the call went through.

A woman answered and Lauren reserved a room for Thursday night, with an open end for departure. The woman asked if she knew there was no snow in Silver Creek, and when she assured her she did, the reservation was made. She put away her phone, then pulled back onto the street.

She went past Rusty's Diner and the SUV was gone. But that was fine because she'd found a chink in Duncan Bishop's facade of power and control, a very unexpected chink. It didn't fit the image in the newspaper clips and stories that she'd read about him. Or from what his father said, or anyone else she'd asked about him. It didn't fit at all, but she'd seen it with her own eyes.

Duncan Bishop was a rescuer. He'd rescued that girl from the gang of obnoxious punks. He hadn't hesitated. Maybe he was more a controller than a rescuer, but whatever it was, it could work for her. If he liked being in control and rescuing maidens in distress, she'd be a maiden, she'd be in distress and she'd let him have control.

Thursday:

"So, you went to Las Vegas, not to gamble, not to have a good time, but to…"

"Business," Duncan said to his passenger in the SUV as he drove into the mountains.

"Business," Annie Logan repeated. "Business?"

Annie owned and ran the Silver Creek Hotel, where he stayed, and he liked her and her husband, Rick. They were nice, uncomplicated people who were generous and kind to a complete stranger. But they never stopped asking questions. That and his overwhelming need for solitude had been why he'd hesitated to let her ride along on his trip to Las Vegas.

But he'd finally agreed to take her so that she could visit with her sister while he took care of business. He hadn't elaborated on what he was doing there, and wasn't going to go into what he'd accomplished in Las Vegas. He'd go over that with Rusty when he got back. The meeting with a restaurant supplier he'd known for years, Colin Webb of Webb Food Services, had gone very well.

Colin was one of the few business acquaintances he'd had over the years who neither feared nor kowtowed to D. R. Bishop. That fact alone had earned him Duncan's respect. On top of that, Colin was a fair man. When Duncan had contacted him last week about helping Rusty get a better deal on his supplies, the only thing Colin had said about him leaving Bishop International was "What took you so long?"

After meeting in Las Vegas to talk, they'd struck a

deal for Rusty's Diner. Colin's company supplied the inn, and it wouldn't take much more to make a stop at Rusty's to take him supplies. The deal was struck, and Duncan was going back to Silver Creek with the good news that deliveries would start the week of Thanksgiving.

"You are not a talker, are you?" Annie asked as she reached for the newspaper on the seat between them.

He shrugged. "It depends." He glanced at the woman in the next seat. Annie was in her early thirties, with dark hair she wore short and curly, little to no makeup, and a woman who wore sensible clothes and shoes. She had a terrific smile and a natural maternal instinct that, without having children, was directed at the people who stayed at the hotel.

"Well, you're an enigma," she said. "I told Rick that there's more to you than meets the eye."

"No, there isn't," he murmured.

He heard the newspaper Annie brought with her rustle, and she read, "Crisis in the national forests. Seems that people are killing the forests. I can't imagine what Silver Creek would be without the forest."

Neither could Duncan. The few days he'd thought he'd spend in Silver Creek had stretched out into three months, and he found he was starting to feel more and more comfortable in the town. He liked the pace, the people, especially the old-timers who were a far cry from the people who had surrounded him in Los Angeles. And he liked the land around him.

He flipped on the headlights of the SUV as he climbed higher into the mountains. It was barely four-thirty, but dusk was lying heavily all around. "Do you think there's snow coming?" he asked for something to say.

"We always have snow by Thanksgiving," Annie said. "And the weather report says we might get some activity. I sure hope so."

He'd guess the temperature outside had dropped ten degrees, but the sky was painfully clear. Annie read more headlines, and he wasn't particularly paying any attention until she said, "Business seems to be as depressing as the conditions in the forest."

"Yeah," he murmured, asking no questions.

But that didn't stop Annie from reading more, and everything he'd avoided for six months hit him in the face. And it hit hard. "Tellgare files for bankruptcy. Stocks plummet. Rivals move in. Sounds like some sharks circling the dead or dying."

That was closer than she thought, and he looked over at her as she refolded the paper. Sickness hit him hard. His father had destroyed Tellgare. He turned his attention back to the road and realized that he'd wandered onto the shoulder. The tires beat on gravel, the three-foot-high wooden safety rail was close and was the only thing to stop a fifty-foot plunge into a rough ravine below.

He tried not to overcorrect, but to ease his way back onto the road. But he didn't have time to do it properly. At the same time as Annie said, "Look out!" he saw a disabled car on the shoulder, right in his path. Its hood was up and its taillights on.

He had no choice but to jerk the wheel to the left,

back toward the pavement. He felt his wheels spin, then grind in the gravel, shooting rocks everywhere as he slipped past the parked car, barely missing impact. But his relief was short-lived when he felt the back end of the SUV start to fishtail wildly, pushing him into a spin. He steered into it, the world outside a blur and Annie's screams ringing in his ears. The SUV rammed the safety rail, then an explosion and the sound of tearing metal, acrid smoke everywhere, and with a shuddering finality, everything stopped.

Chapter Three

Lauren saw the SUV come out of nowhere, headed right for her, then, in a surreal moment, it passed by her. Before she could blink, the SUV started to spin, throwing gravel back at her car. Dust rose and the SUV slammed into the safety rail sideways, skidded along the barrier, then stopped in a cloud of dust. In that moment she realized the black SUV belonged to Duncan Bishop.

She was out of her car in an instant, running toward the SUV, coughing from the dust and the smell of burning rubber. She reached the driver's side, grabbed the door handle and pulled, but it was locked. She pounded on the window, calling out, "Open it, open it, open it!" The door flew back suddenly, almost hitting her before she could jump out of the way.

Then she saw Duncan Bishop. The air bag had ruptured from the center of the steering wheel and the smell of chemicals all but choked her. She grabbed his jacket sleeve, the idea that she nearly got him killed too unbelievable to absorb. "Oh, my gosh, are you okay?"

she said, the words spilling out over each other. She let go of his arm. "My gosh, I thought you were going to go over the edge."

"Me, too," he muttered as he twisted toward her to get out of the SUV. His feet hit the ground, and she backed up to give him space. He towered over her.

"You just skidded, I mean, the SUV was going all over and I thought—"

"I know what you thought," he said, straightening in the cold air. "And it's my fault."

"Oh, no, if I hadn't parked my car there, you never would have—"

"I got distracted," he said.

"I can't open the door." A voice came from the car and the next thing Lauren knew, a woman had slid across the driver's seat and gotten out.

She was of medium height, slender, almost plain. Certainly not an Adrianna Barr type. The woman pressed a hand to her chest and gasped, "Oh, my goodness, now that was a ride."

Duncan asked if she was okay then headed to the hood of the SUV. Lauren followed. Together they stared at the damage. The front tire on the passenger side was torn to bits and the rim had dug into the gravel. The SUV was butted up against the guardrail. Deep ruts were embedded in the body thanks to the large metal bolts that held the wooden rails in place.

"Holy cow," she whispered and Duncan turned, almost hitting her in the chin with his arm. She moved back quickly. This was not how the plan was supposed to go. "You really did wreck your car, didn't you?"

"That about sums it up," he said. "That tire's history and we're stuck."

"No, no, we'll put on your spare, and we'll be fine."

"No, the spare's gone."

The SUV was so new it didn't even have its regular plates on yet. Lauren had to crook her neck slightly to look up at him. "You don't have a spare?"

"I tore up a tire a week ago on a strip of metal in the road, and I haven't picked up the replacement yet."

The mystery woman appeared, pressing herself between Duncan and Lauren to take a long look at the damage. Then she drew back and looked up at Duncan. "And you don't have a spare?"

"Ladies, there is no spare tire," he said with a touch of exasperation. He glanced back down the road where Lauren had parked. "What's wrong with your car?"

She stuck with the words she'd rehearsed while she'd been waiting for him to show up, when she'd hoped he'd stop to rescue another damsel in distress. "It stalled and I can't get it started, and my cell phone has no signal."

He exhaled, his breath curling into the cold air. "Let's see if I can't get your car started."

But as he made his way toward her vehicle, Lauren followed and blocked his path. "I can't let you mess with that car. It's a classic. It's not just some old car."

In fact, the car was her brother's, almost forty years old, completely restored, and recently had a new paint job that Alan called "cherry-apple red." It had taken real bribery to get him to part with it for a week or so, and let her drive it all the way here. But she knew she'd need a car that wouldn't be overlooked or forgotten by Duncan. "And it's really temperamental." That was true, and it was also true that if he knew anything about old cars, he'd know that the coil wire had been pulled out. "It's got a mind of its own."

He almost laughed at her. "It's a car, lady."

She stood her ground. "It's my car," she said. "I'll take care of it."

"You said it stopped, and you couldn't get it going. Why do you think you can fix it now?"

"No, I said it stalled and I parked here," she said, quickly elaborating to cover her tracks. "I didn't get to finish and tell you that sometimes, if you let it rest for a bit, it'll start."

Damn it, he was going to laugh, really laugh. She could see it in the failing light. "So, it's pouting, and won't go until you make nice-nice to it?"

She didn't smile. "No, it's got a problem with the electrical wiring, and sometimes it reconnects and restarts."

"Let her try," the woman said as she came up behind Duncan and grabbed his arm. "It's freezing and we have to get back."

He pushed his hands into his jacket pockets and nodded to the car. "Go ahead and talk to it nicely and make it understand that we need to have a ride out of here."

Lauren didn't wait to be asked twice. She hurried to the car and made a show of tinkering under the hood before reconnecting the wires. Standing, she turned to look at the other two. "That should do it, if we're lucky."

"A lady who can fix her own car," the woman said approvingly. "I love it."

Lauren reached up to pull the hood closed, then she went around to get behind the wheel. She waited a moment, then turned the key and the strong engine kicked over immediately. Her brother had completely rebuilt the engine and it worked perfectly. She turned on the headlights, drove slowly forward and came even with Duncan as she rolled down the window. "You two need a ride?"

"You're terrific," the woman said.

Duncan said, "Annie, get in, and I'll get our things from the car." He headed back to the disabled SUV while the woman, Annie, ran around the front of the car and pulled the passenger door open.

She scrambled into the back seat. "Duncan would never fit back here," she said as she sank onto the white tuck-and-roll upholstery.

"Sorry it's so small back there," Lauren said and saw the emergency flashers of the SUV click on. Duncan got back out, closed up the car, then headed back to them with a small bag in one hand and a large envelope in the other. He went around and climbed in, taking the other bucket seat and quickly closing the door after him. He gave Annie the small bag and kept the envelope. "Got everything?" she asked.

He glanced at her and skimmed off his watch cap. His hair spiked slightly around his face, and she could see the beginnings of a beard at his jawline. A rough version of his father, very rough. "I left the luggage. We can get it later," he said, then asked, "Is it going to keep running?"

"I hope so." She eased out onto the highway.

"This is a great car," Annie said, sitting forward to lean between the bucket seats. "And I'm Annie Logan."

"I'm Lauren," she said and waited for Duncan to chime in. He didn't.

Instead, he asked, "Where were you heading, Lauren?"

She started her cover story. "Up the road a ways."

"Is that a gypsy thing?" he asked.

"Do I look like a gypsy?" she asked.

"I don't know."

She pushed back the hood of the lime-green jacket she'd chosen to make an impact, then glanced at him. "I've got freckles and red hair. Gypsies don't usually have either trait."

He was studying her intently. "I guess not," he murmured.

"Now, where am I taking the two of you?"

"Up the road."

Annie jumped in. "Don't pay any attention to him. Getting information out of him is like pulling teeth. We're going to Silver Creek."

The fact that Duncan Bishop was with a woman shouldn't have surprised Lauren, not after what his father had told her and what she knew from the checks she'd done into his romantic history. But the type of woman surprised her. Annie Logan seemed warm and friendly, and unassuming. Lauren doubted anyone would have called Adrianna Barr unassuming. She shot Annie a glance in the rearview mirror and said, "Silver Creek it is."

"Have you ever been there?" Duncan asked.

"No," she lied. "Why?"

"I thought you looked familiar, but I guess not."

She looked familiar? He couldn't remember her from that flashing moment in the diner. He'd barely looked at her, and she'd done everything to be invisible, down to wearing dark clothes and that stupid knit hat. "I guess I've got that kind of face."

"What kind?"

"The kind where you think you saw me before, but you couldn't have, because I was never where you thought I was, so you couldn't have seen me."

"Whew, I can't argue with that reasoning," he said.

The car surged slightly, mostly because her foot jerked on the gas. "Sorry, sometimes it's a little—"

"I know, temperamental," Duncan finished for her.

Lauren nibbled on her bottom lip as she drove up the grade. Okay, so instead of him doing the rescuing when her car broke down, she'd been the one to rescue him…sort of. She regretted that his SUV was the worse for wear, but she'd made so certain she'd pulled over in a safe spot. Lots of shoulder area. And he should have seen her in this car with its red paint and the parking lights on.

Even though she didn't know how he could have almost hit her, she took the blame to get talking again. "I'm sorry I parked where I did and almost got you both killed."

She felt him shift, and she knew he was looking right at her. "I crashed because I was trying to miss your car, but then again, if the car hadn't been there, I might have kept going and gone right over the rail. I'd say this is the better scenario."

She shivered at the thought of that happening, and for a moment she thought of her job, of the consequences that came from every action she took to do things right. Thank goodness the consequences this time were relatively minor. And she was with Duncan Bishop. "Much better."

"Thank goodness we didn't go over," Annie said. "And thank goodness you got your car going."

"So, how did you get this car going?" Duncan asked.

"There's a wire that goes to the coil, and it…it can come out pretty easily." She'd barely had to tug to free it after she'd parked on the shoulder.

"It just slipped out of place?"

"I guess so," she lied. Being the youngest in a family with three brothers had been rough, but it did have its advantages when it came to disabling a car.

"And this happens a lot?" Annie asked.

"Off and on," she said, looking ahead intently, and not chancing a look at the man close to her.

"Why haven't you had it fixed?" Duncan asked—the same thing she would have asked.

She took a breath, taking her boss's advice and sticking to the truth as much as possible when you weave a backstory on assignment. The theory was, you had less to remember, and less to fabricate. "The car was rewired when the engine was rebuilt, and I guess that the new wires were just that, new. And the car's old. The match isn't perfect." He didn't comment, so she guessed he bought the explanation. Her hands tightened on the steering wheel and she tried to reroute the conversation. "You live in Silver Creek?"

"We both do," Annie said before Duncan could say anything.

Annie was making this difficult, a talker who picked up when Duncan hesitated for any reason. So she tried to work around that by glancing at Duncan and making eye contact so he knew she was talking to him. "You like it?" she asked.

As she looked back at the road, he said, "Sure."

One-word answers weren't what she'd hoped for, so she regrouped and said, "You never told me your name."

"Duncan," he said, and that was that.

He didn't say anything else, but Annie did, chattering on about Silver Creek and how she'd lived there all her life. She never said how she knew Duncan, but told her everything else about the town. She would have made a good tour guide, Lauren thought, trying not to be annoyed with the woman. She listened, waiting for Annie to stop. They were less than five miles from the town, and the glow from the ski slopes was starting to show in the night sky. Once they got there, she knew he'd be out of the car and gone before she could say goodbye.

"Duncan," she said when Annie took a breath, trying to find something to say as she tapped the top of the steering wheel with the tip of her forefinger. Then she heard herself saying something totally ludicrous, but she couldn't take it back once it was out there. "So, are you a highlander?"

"What?"

She looked at him, making a smile form on her lips. "A Scottish highlander. You're in the right setting, a wild, cold country. Like the Highlands of Scotland, and your name, Duncan, it fits."

"Sorry, my mother was Irish, and my father is…" He hesitated, then finally said, "Whatever he wants to be."

D. R. Bishop *would* be whatever he wanted to be. That was dead on. "Good or bad?" she asked, hoping to get him to talk a bit about his father, but he gave his usual condensed one- or two-word answer.

"That depends."

Thankfully, Annie had sat back in her seat, apparently gathering her strength for another bout of conversation. So Lauren kept going, trying to get Duncan to say something she could connect with. "So, are you a ski champion or something?"

"No."

"I thought with all the snow and cold, that being a skier around here was a no-brainer."

"There isn't any snow," Annie said, active again as she sat forward. "Not a flake. Nothing."

Lauren glanced at the woman in her rearview mirror, then at Duncan. His eyes were narrowed on her, a look he shared with his father, that way of studying what was in front of him intently, and intensely. "There's no snow?" she asked, the lament that had been everywhere on her short visit to Silver Creek.

Annie jumped in again, earnestly saying, "It's the driest season yet, and the slopes are all being filled by machine." She said that as if it were something horrible. "The skiing's just awful, and the slopes are all but shut down."

"What about that fancy resort?"

"They can have snow in July up there," she said.

"I guess money buys just about anything," she said, waiting to see how Duncan responded.

He didn't. Annie did, giving a long tirade about how the resort had tried to eat up the town, and how it drew so many outsiders. But not once had Annie said anything personal to Duncan. There hadn't been any "connection" between them, no touching, no smiles, nothing intimate at all. And Lauren wondered what they were to each other. Obviously they were close enough to go to Las Vegas together, but there was something missing between them.

"Do you need me to take you someplace to get your car towed?" she asked Duncan.

"Rollie's Garage on the main street," he said. "It's just as you get into the old section of town."

Lauren was tired of all this dancing around with words and decided time was short, so she went for a direct hit. "So, how long have you been in Silver Creek, Duncan?"

She felt Duncan look back at her, but it was Annie who spoke up once again, answering for him. "He walked in two, maybe three months ago. He came and never left."

That told her nothing, except that there were three or four months unaccounted for. She stared ahead at the glow from the ski runs that was spreading in the dusky sky. Talking to Duncan with Annie around was next to useless, and she figured she had to take a different tack before the car stopped at Rollie's Garage.

They were close to town now, going past the first

scattering of houses digging into the foothills at the base of the soaring mountains on either side, their lights flashing in the night. Then more buildings, a huge stone structure to the right with a lit sign near the road, Silver Creek Clinic. A few small businesses were closing for the day at the beginning of the main street. The old-fashioned lampposts lined the way, and the Christmas lights twinkled everywhere.

"There's Rollie's," Annie said, motioning just ahead of them to the left.

Lauren saw the sign set between the street and an island of gas pumps. Beyond the pumps was an older building with a false-wood fronted office and to the right, three service bays with their metal doors closed tightly. A neon red Closed sign shone in the window of the office.

"It's closed," Lauren said, grateful for the opportunity to buy more time and take Duncan to another garage.

"Just pull in. He's there," Duncan said, so she had no choice but to swing off the street and over toward the office.

She had to think fast because otherwise she'd lose even this weak connection. So she kept talking, making every attempt to draw him into a meaningful conversation. "The town is bigger than I thought it would be."

"It's huge," Annie said. "Just huge. When I was growing up, there were only two hundred residents, and now look at it. Although it's not all residents, not at all. I mean, I told you about the influx of all those people for skiing and the rich ones who go straight through and hide behind the walls at the inn."

She'd told her that three times, Lauren thought, but who was keeping count? She stopped by the door of the closed offices, let the car idle and spoke off the top of her head to buy time. "I'll wait for you."

"You don't have to," Duncan said, his hand on the door handle. "We can walk."

"Oh, no," she said, glancing at Annie to include her in what she said, hoping she'd help her this time. "I can't just drop the two of you off here."

But Annie wasn't an ally this time. "We'll be just fine," Annie said quickly, before Duncan could respond. "We're just going down the street a bit."

While Annie spoke, Duncan opened his door to get out, and Lauren did the same thing. She knew Annie was scrambling out of the back, then heard the door close, but she never took her eyes off Duncan who was striding to the offices. She caught up with him as he raised his hand to rap on the glass window.

"You don't know for sure if anyone's in there, and I feel responsible. It's so cold, and—"

He looked down at her, his face shadowed by the lights behind him. "Rollie is here twenty-four seven."

"But he's not here. It looks empty," she said.

"He lives out the back. He'll be here," he said and rapped on the window, harder this time.

"You could have whiplash or something." She spoke quickly, and included Annie in what she was saying. "You could both have whiplash."

He rotated his head, then shrugged. "Nothing."

And, damn it, Annie chimed in, cheerfully saying, "I'm just fine."

"Well, the car's all messed up, and I feel as if I'm responsible for that."

He narrowed his eyes even more. "You've got an overdeveloped guilt complex, don't you?"

If she did, she wouldn't be playing this game with him. "I just believe in taking responsibility."

Annie patted her arm. "Oh, it's not your responsibility. If anything, I was reading that darn newspaper to him about the national forests being in trouble, then businesses going belly up. I'm the one at fault if you want to lay blame."

A light inside flashed on without warning and its glow exposed the face of Duncan Bishop. His father's son. The same look. No neatly trimmed beard or white hair, but the strong features, the dark-as-night eyes and a size that seemed almost overwhelming. He turned to the window, exposing his profile and a peculiar arrogance in the way he held his jaw. Like his father. But the rough clothes weren't like D.R.'s expensive, tailored suits, and for him to be standing in front of a gas station waiting for help wasn't like his father at all.

Lauren turned to the light and saw the office was just a small room, cut in two from side to side by a scarred counter, and with walls lined with oils and greases and small car parts. A single figure was coming around the counter, a man of medium height, unremarkable in greasy overalls and with little hair on his head. He squinted at the three of them through the hazy glass, then reached for the door and unlocked it.

"Duncan? What's going on?" he asked as the barrier swung open.

"I almost went off the road back down the way near Elder's Curve. It tore up my tire and cut into the side of the car."

"An accident?" he asked as his gaze flicked from Annie to Lauren, then back to Duncan. "Are you all okay?"

"We're fine, Rollie," Annie said for all three of them. "And I'm late." She looked at Duncan. "I'll get my bag out of the car and walk on home. Thanks for an interesting trip."

He nodded. "I'll be along as soon as I take care of this."

Annie touched Lauren on the arm. "Nice running into you," she said, then realized what she'd said and laughed out loud. "Didn't mean that," she said. "But it was nice meeting you."

She went back to the idling car, got her bag out, then with a wave, she took off down the street. "I should have driven her," Lauren said.

"She's not going far," Rollie said. "She's used to Silver Creek. Been here all her life." He looked to Lauren again, then past her to her car. "This car was in an accident?"

"No, I swerved to miss hitting it, and went off the road," Duncan said.

Rollie went toward the car, reached out and touched the fender reverently. Then he grinned back at Duncan. "Well, damn it, man, aren't we all thankful you didn't scratch her up? What a beauty," he said in a low voice, then leaned down as if listening to the engine. "She's got a V-8, overhead, don't she?" he asked Lauren as he straightened up.

"Completely rebuilt," Lauren said.

He stood back. "Not original paint, is it?"

"No, it's redone."

He emitted a low whistle as he slowly circled the car. "Great job." He came back around to where they stood in the cold. "Where'd you get her?" he asked Lauren.

"My uncle bought it new, and my brother restored it a year or so ago."

"He's a gifted man," Rollie said.

"Rollie," Duncan said, interrupting the man's rapture over the car. "Do you think you can tear yourself away to get the tire?"

"Oh, yeah," Rollie said, as if he'd forgotten Duncan existed for a moment. "You coming with me?"

"Yeah."

"Okay, give me a minute, and I'll be right out," Rollie said. But he didn't go inside right away. Instead, he looked back to Lauren. "You want to sell that baby?"

"No, I sure don't," she said.

"Then you take good care of her, hear?" he said, and headed right back inside.

She was thankful Annie had taken off, but now Duncan was about to leave, too, to get his car. She looked at him and was taken aback to find the shadow of a smile playing at the corners of his wide mouth. "I think Rollie's in love."

Rollie returned before she could absorb the expression on Duncan's face. Before she could be sure if she saw a faint dimple to one side of his mouth. Rollie hurried out, closed the door and tugged his heavy coat around him. "Okay, let's hit the road," he said to Duncan.

"Okay," Duncan said, then both men were going past the service bays and rounding the corner. Duncan looked back at Lauren with a wave and called, "Thanks," then was gone.

She didn't move. She listened, heard doors open and close, then a big engine roar to life. In a moment a huge pickup truck lumbered into view. She could barely make out the shadows of the two men in the cab, then the truck turned onto the street heading back the way she'd just come.

That was that, at least for now. She hurried to the idling car, drove it back onto the main street and headed north. She went one block, parked and looked at Rusty's Diner. It was time to formulate a new plan. And there was only one thing she could think of to do now.

Chapter Four

It took Duncan an hour to get the tire changed on the SUV, take off some loose metal and drive it back to town. He passed Rollie in the old pickup, hit his horn to thank him again for his trouble, then continued driving to the hotel. He parked in an open spot in front, ran in to clean up, made sure Annie got back okay and gave her the luggage, then headed out again. He left the car parked where it was and walked south, heading for the diner.

And while he walked, he found himself looking at every passing car, in search of Lauren's old car. He didn't see it anywhere, and he wondered if she'd just driven on through and kept going. She didn't seem as if she could afford to stay at the inn, and she hadn't said whether she skied, but without any snow, that didn't matter.

He crossed the street and stepped into the diner, generally noticed it wasn't very busy before he went down the side hallway to the office. The door was ajar. He went in and found Rusty at the desk going over cash register tapes. The older man looked up, the glasses he had to use for reading perched on the end of his nose. "Well, damn, where've you been, boy? You said five and it's going on seven. You had me worried."

"Sorry, I had a flat tire, and no spare. Rollie took care of it for me," he said.

"Another flat?" Rusty asked.

"Yeah, another flat."

Rusty sat back in the chair in the small, cluttered office. The only window was covered with a red-checked curtain, and filing cabinets crowded most of the wall space. Rusty clasped his hands on his stomach. "Any snow out there?"

He shook his head. "No. What's the forecast?"

"Possible snow tonight. If not, by tomorrow sometime. Can't be soon enough for me."

Duncan handed the envelope out to him. "I saw Webb and he cut us a great deal." While Rusty opened it and scanned the figures, Duncan said, "That'll cut twenty-five percent off per quarter."

"I can't thank you enough for this," Rusty said and laid the papers on top of the tapes. "The day you walked in here was my lucky day."

"For both of us," he said.

"Thanks." He exhaled. "I needed good news today."

"What's going on?" Duncan asked as he shrugged out of his heavy jacket and hung it on a hook by the door.

"The grill's acting up again, Shannon, the morning waitress, her kid's misbehaving, so she'll be off for at least a week." He exhaled. "I knew there was a reason I never had any of those little humans."

Duncan tugged off his watch cap and stuffed it in the pocket of his hanging jacket. "What about Arlene?"

"She can't pull too many double shifts. Damn, she's near my age." He stood. "Don't you go worrying, though. I had one stroke of good luck today, besides your deal. A girl walked in right off the streets asking for a job."

"I hope she works out."

"Well, she's done waitressing for three, four years, mostly stuff like we have here, and she's only sticking around for a few weeks. Fits perfectly."

Duncan unbuttoned the cuffs of his red plaid shirt and rolled up his sleeves. "Webb says he'll start delivery in two days. He supplies the big place up on the hill, so supplying you's just a matter of another stop in town. He just needs you to call in the order to the warehouse."

Rusty reached for the envelope. "I'll get right on it."

"I'll go and check on the grill."

Duncan left the office, intending to go to the kitchen and check the supplies there, but he never made it past the dining room. The chime sounded for the front door, and Lauren stepped in. She stopped, straightened, pushed off her hood and saw him.

Her eyes were lavender, wide and darkly lashed, and her hair was a deep red, just this side of auburn, feathered around her finely boned face that had, as she'd said, its share of freckles. But there was a bit of a tan, too, and color dotted her cheeks from the cold. Her lips seemed pale, but seductively full. He hadn't been able to see her all that well in the car, but she'd seemed familiar. Now, as she stood there, he knew he'd seen her before.

Not the car, not that hair, but those eyes. Definitely. He just couldn't remember where. "Well, what a surprise," she murmured as she slipped off her bright, lime-green jacket. He saw the swell of her full breasts under a plain white shirt, and the flare of seductively curved hips under well-worn jeans. Her heavy boots had been replaced by running shoes.

Duncan realized she was staring at him and that she'd spoken to him. And for the first time in as long as he could remember, Duncan felt tongue-tied around a woman. She saved him from looking totally stupid by coming closer. "Duncan?" she asked, putting her jacket over one arm. "I never thought I'd find you here. What happened with your car?"

"It's running on a new tire," he finally said.

She grimaced. "Was the damage as bad as it looked?"

"Bad enough."

Those incredible eyes held his gaze and he had the passing thought that the color couldn't be real. It had to be enhanced by tinted contacts or something. "Sorry about that."

"I have a few questions," Rusty said as he came up behind Duncan and touched his arm. "I was wondering—"

His words were cut off when the door flew open, cold air rushed into the restaurant and a kid who worked at the coffee shop across the street ran inside. "Snow!" he announced in a loud voice. "It's finally here, and it's going to keep snowing for a while." He was dark and small, dressed in an all-brown uniform, but his smile was huge. "Snow at last!"

Rusty pushed past Duncan, glanced at Lauren and said, "We've got snow," and went outside after the kid. Lauren and Duncan followed. They stopped at the edge of the walkway and watched as huge, soft flakes fell from the black, black sky, silently drifting onto the streets of Silver Creek. They clung to everything, making a pale haze on the parked cars and dancing past the glow of the street lamps. Snow.

Lauren still had her jacket on one arm, and she held her other hand out, palm up. She watched the huge flakes fall on her skin and melt instantly from the heat. She looked awestruck.

"We're in business," Rusty was saying. "In business...finally."

"I'd say so," Duncan murmured, but kept watching Lauren tip her face to the heavens and touch her tongue to her lips when snow brushed the pale-pink fullness.

"Wow," she breathed softly.

He couldn't remember the last time he'd looked at a woman and simply wanted her. No questions asked. Just wanted her. "Your first snow?" he asked, getting a bit closer to her.

"No." Her eyes stayed on the falling snow for a long moment, then she turned to him, hugging her jacket to her middle. "But it's just so incredible."

"It's money in the bank," Rusty said heartily, then startled Duncan by coming over to Lauren and taking her by her arm. The next thing he knew, Rusty was tugging her toward the still open door. "Come on. We need to get moving. Things are going to get crazy now."

Duncan didn't know why Rusty had taken Lauren's

arm, or why she was going with him as if it were just fine by her. He went inside and caught up with the two. "We're in business, boy, and it's going to be good." Then he looked at Lauren. "Good timing. I was wondering when you'd get back."

Get back? She'd been here before?

"I had to get my things to my room," she was saying. "And I had to get settled."

Settled? Her room? She was staying in Silver Creek? She hadn't mentioned that on the ride.

"Come on," Rusty said, motioning her to follow him as he started into the hallway. He cast a fleeting glance back at Duncan. "You, too."

Duncan did as he was told, following the two of them down the hallway, inches behind Lauren. The scent he'd detected in her car faintly touched the air as she and Rusty made their way into the office.

"What's going on?" Duncan asked as Rusty dropped onto his chair and reached for a notepad to his right.

The man looked up. "I told you, I hired a new waitress." He motioned to Lauren. "Meet Lauren Carter. Lauren, this is Duncan Bishop. He hangs out here when he wants to. Helps me conduct business."

He looked at Lauren as she turned those lavender eyes in his direction. "You're a waitress?"

"I am now." She shifted her jacket to her left hand, then reached with her right into the pocket of her jeans. She took out a folded sheet of paper and reached across the desk to hand it to Rusty. "Here's the references I promised."

He took the paper and scanned it. "Some nice places."

"It's all the same work," she said. "Get food to the customer and make them happy."

"Ain't that the truth." Rusty looked at Duncan. "I'd say this was our lucky day."

Duncan looked at Lauren again, meeting the gaze from those eyes, and spoke with plain truthfulness. "A very lucky day."

Lauren saw the surprise in Duncan's dark eyes at her being their new waitress. Truth be told, she was surprised, too. She hadn't known she was going to do this until she saw the Help Wanted sign in the front window. She went in, and before she knew it, she'd taken a shot in the dark in an attempt to get closer to Duncan Bishop, and it had paid off.

She'd worked her way through college and the first year of law school as a waitress before she got hired on at Sutton. Now she was going to be a waitress for a few days again. That was the easy part. She'd checked into the Silver Creek Hotel, sat down to work out a bogus list of references, and even set things up so that if Rusty checked, all phone numbers would lead to a phone line at her office. But she doubted he'd even check her work history. This was what she was counting on.

"It's my lucky day, too," she said to both men.

Rusty glanced at Duncan. "Why don't you show her around the kitchen? I left her an apron out there on the hook by the door." He looked back to Lauren. "Hang your jacket there," he said, motioning to pegs by the door.

After hanging up her jacket, she followed Duncan out through the restaurant and into the kitchen. She almost ran into his broad back when he stopped suddenly, and called across the kitchen to the cook who was chopping vegetables by the stove and to a young kid washing dishes. "This is Lauren, the new waitress."

The cook was the one she'd seen the first time she'd been to Rusty's, with a full mustache and a baseball cap worn backward. He smiled at her and showed a missing front tooth. "I'm Mo, and anything you need, you just ask."

"Thanks," she said.

The kid was maybe fifteen or sixteen, skinny, with long dark hair. He barely nodded to her before going back to the dishes. "He's Phoenix," Duncan said.

She looked back at Duncan. "Rusty didn't say anything about a uniform except to wear comfortable shoes." She wiggled one foot. "Got the shoes. Do I need anything else?"

"No, you're fine," he said and she saw that extra second of hesitation before he asked, "Why didn't you tell me you were looking for a job?"

She had his interest, even if it was one tinged with a bit of suspicion. "Why didn't you tell me you worked here?"

"Why would I?"

"Exactly," she said.

"Touché."

She glanced around the kitchen, a not overly large area, but one that looked well equipped and efficient. "So, what else do I need to know about working here?"

"It's hard work," he said.

"I can handle it."

His eyes narrowed on her. "I guess we'll find that out, won't we?"

Rusty came into the kitchen. "Sorry. I thought I left the apron in here for you, but I didn't." He handed her a navy apron that was the size of a fanny pack with four pockets. "The ticket book and a pen are in one pocket. Any questions about the menu, just ask anyone."

"Okay," she said as she took the things, slipped on the small blue apron, adjusted it and found the new ticket book, pen and some straws in the pockets. "I'm as ready as I'll ever be," she said.

"You've got the booths on the side wall, and tables six through ten. Now, go on out there and smile. I've got a feeling we'll be bustling before too long." He glanced at the clock. "We're open until eleven, and it's going to be busy."

She glanced at Duncan, but he was reading a supply list by the doors. With a nod to Rusty, she went through the swinging door and into the dining room. She felt pretty good about the way things had gone. Her plan might just work. She was here. Duncan was here, and when he got back to his room, she'd be there, too. Her room at the hotel was right next to his. That had been really good luck.

Now, she just had to be everywhere Duncan was, get to know him and be patient. She smiled as she approached a couple who were just taking a seat in one of the booths. "Good evening," she said. "My name's Lauren and I'll be your server this evening."

They actually didn't lock the front door of Rusty's until midnight, and when the last customer finally filed out, Lauren was exhausted. Her feet hurt. Her back hurt. Her arms hurt, and she had a raging headache. It had been a while since she'd done any waitressing and she'd all but forgotten how hard it could be. Smile, be polite, remember every menu change and make the customer happy. That was hard, hard work.

As the other waitress, Arlene, locked the front door, Lauren looked around and saw Rusty in the kitchen with the cook by the grill. Phoenix had left two hours ago without a word to anyone. Duncan had left without her seeing him go. She hadn't realized he was gone until Rusty had told her, "He won't be back tonight."

Lauren sank onto the end stool at the now vacant counter and pulled her tips out of her apron pocket. She dropped the bills and coins on the green Formica top. An impressive pile. "Well, well, well," she sighed, "I haven't lost my touch." The tips were good, very good, and an unexpected bonus.

"Did you survive?" Rusty asked from behind her.

She swivelled around to face him. "I think so."

"Terrific, because we'll be like this from now on, with the snow and all. The big restaurants get most of the fancy lunch and dinner business, and we get all the in-between types." He studied her. "Are you beat, or could you possibly come in for the breakfast and early lunch shift tomorrow? With the lifts up, everyone and their uncle will want something hot."

She didn't know if she could stand again, but she didn't hesitate. "I'll work whatever schedule you need me to work."

"That's music to my ears. You're damn good at this."

"Thanks," she said and turned to gather up her money and put it back in her apron pocket. "Is there anything else I need to do before leaving?"

"No, not tonight. I'll take care of things for the morning."

She slipped off the stool and got ready to head out, then asked, "What time tomorrow?"

"Six-thirty."

Way too early, she thought, but said, "See you then. I just need to get my jacket."

"I'll get it for you," Rusty said, and before she could stop him, he hurried off toward the office.

She glanced at the kitchen through the pass-through window and saw Duncan talking to the cook again. She thought he'd left. He never looked up, and when Rusty came back with her jacket, she was ready to leave. "Just use the front door. It locks automatically," Rusty told her.

She headed for the door, shrugged into her jacket, then stepped out and pulled the door shut behind her. The snow was coming down heavily now, drifting past the glow of the street lamps, covering the cars by the curb, all but hiding them, and starting to alter the look of the old buildings. She did up her jacket, then pushed her hands into her pockets, hunched into the cold and headed down the street.

By the time she stepped into the warm air in the lobby of the old hotel, she was half-frozen. Her feet were wet from snow falling into her running shoes, her face ached and her nose felt as if it would start running any minute. She stamped her feet to try to free the cling-ing snow on a huge mat laid over the well-worn wooden floors in the old-fashioned lobby, then started for the stairs that lead up to her room.

"Lauren?" She turned and was shocked to see Annie Logan coming out of a downstairs hallway. "What are you doing here?"

Annie lived here? "I'm staying here," she said, too tired for Annie's chatter and looking for a way to cut this short and get to her room. "I was just going up to my room."

Annie was right by her, still smiling, her hyper energy still intact even after midnight. "Oh, my gosh, you're L. Carter?"

"What?"

"On the check-in sheet, I saw L. Carter and Wendell said he'd taken care of you. It was you all along." She grinned as if she'd won the lottery. "Who would have thought?"

"Yeah, who would have?" she murmured with a great deal less enthusiasm than Annie.

"Wow, wait until Duncan finds out that—"

"He already knows I'm here, at least in town," she said quickly. "I'm working at Rusty's."

No questions about how or why, Annie just said enthusiastically, "Wow, that's really terrific. You're staying for a while?"

"Until I make a bit of money," she said and barely covered a yawn. "I have to get up early and I'm beat."

"Oh, sure. Let me know if you need anything?"

She worked here as a maid? "No, I don't think so."

"Well, if you do, just ring the desk. I'll be right there, at least, once I wake up, I'll be there."

"You work the night shift?"

That smile came back. "I work every shift. My husband, Rick, and I own the hotel."

Her husband? "Your husband and you own it?"

"We bought it when we got married. They were putting in the resort up the hill, and there was talk about turning this building into a health club." She shook her head. "We decided to save it from that fate, buy it and run it."

Lauren barely covered a yawn again, and Annie said quickly, "Oh, you go on upstairs and we'll talk at breakfast. It's served beginning at six in the back dining room."

She nodded, but had no intention of chatting that early. "I'll see you tomorrow," she said and headed for the stairs.

Duncan had gone to Las Vegas with his landlady? She couldn't begin to sort that out when she was so tired. She slowly made her way up the stairs to her room. She put the old-fashioned key in the lock and went into the shadowy room. Stripping off her clothes without bothering with the light, she padded into the bathroom to turn on the hot water in the shower that hooked out over an old-fashioned, claw-foot bathtub.

She went back into the bedroom to get her shampoo and heard a knock on her door. "Yes?"

"It's me, Annie."

All she wanted to do was say, "Go away," but instead she called out, "Just a minute," snapped on a side light and pulled her bag she'd left on the floor up onto the bed. She took out her robe, slipped it on, then cinched it at her waist as she went barefoot to the door. She partly opened it and looked out.

It was Annie, all right, but for once she wasn't smiling. That seemed about as odd to her as palm trees in the Arctic. An unsmiling Annie, and an Annie who said without preamble, "I need to talk to you right now."

Chapter Five

"Excuse me?" Lauren asked, but had the feeling there was trouble coming. "What's going on?"

She didn't miss the way Annie was clasping her hands tightly in front of her. "This place, I told you Rick and I run it, and we have for eight years, and we have regulars who come every year for the skiing. They love what they call the 'quaint' experience of staying here." She spoke so quickly that Lauren almost couldn't understand her. "When there was no snow, all bets were off. The regulars don't come near the town. But now that there's snow, and it looks as if it's going to keep snowing for a while, and the skiing will be terrific, things have changed."

Lauren had no use for a rundown on how the snow affected Annie's business. Maybe the woman was losing it. "What are you talking about?"

"Well, Lauren, this is the way it is. There's a couple who always rent out the same room, but they're getting a divorce. The husband still wants to come on up, and he wants his room."

Shoot. She was finally following Annie. "My room is the room they used to have, and now he wants it for himself?"

"Sick, isn't it?" Annie asked with a grimace. "But true."

"You want me to change rooms?"

"Oh, if you could, it would be wonderful. Just wonderful."

"Okay, sure. Just point me to my new room."

"Oh, great." She reached out and gripped Lauren's arm. "Thank you. Thank you."

"No problem," she murmured. "When I checked in, the boy said there were two rooms at the back, by the stairs? One of those?"

"No," she said. "I'm sorry. They were booked this evening, and the people are arriving tomorrow. I only have one room, on the next floor, and there isn't a bathroom in the room. You'd have to use the hall bathroom on this floor by the stairs." She was starting to smile again. "But I could get you a very nice room at another hotel in town. I know a lot of people, and I know I could—"

"No, thanks," she said, ready to sleep in the attic if it meant staying at the hotel. She wouldn't be next to Duncan, but close. "I'll take the room."

"The room's small," she said.

"No problem."

"Don't you want to see it first?"

"Sure, okay," she said. "Let me turn off the shower." She went back in, shut off the hot water, then followed Annie to the end of the hallway. Annie pointed out the bathroom Lauren would have to use, then they headed upstairs. Lauren had to duck to make sure she didn't hit her head on the low beams as she stepped out into a small hallway.

"We're going to remodel soon, and put two rooms up here, but right now, it's raw attic, except for this room that I think used to be the chambermaid's." She unlocked the door to the left, then stepped inside.

Lauren looked in. The room wasn't small, it was minuscule, maybe six feet wide and eight feet long, and where the bed was fitted there was a dormer. It took up a good half of the room. A small dresser to the right, a single straight-backed chair and a nightstand took up the rest of the space. "This is it," Anne said as she turned to Lauren. "As I told you, small and nothing special."

If Lauren had been claustrophobic, she knew she couldn't have stayed here. "It's fine," she said. "I'll get my things together, and—"

"Oh, don't worry about that tonight," Annie said quickly. "The guy won't be here until tomorrow afternoon some time."

"Okay," Lauren said and they headed back to her room. "But I have to go to work early tomorrow. I'll just put my things up here, and clear the other room before I leave."

"You're being so sweet about this, the least I can do is give you a free night and move your things for you," Annie said as they went back down to Lauren's room. "Don't worry about it."

"No, no, it's okay. I'll do it." She reached for her doorknob and turned to look at Annie. "I'll put my things by the door and you can clean around them. I don't have much."

Anne looked past Lauren and her smile came back full force. "Well, hello there. Still snowing?"

"It's not going to stop for a while."

Duncan. She turned and saw him just stepping into the hallway from the stairs, his jacket and watch cap covered with snow and his boots trailing moisture on the hardwood floor.

"Good," Annie said, then glanced over at Lauren before looking at Duncan again. "Can you believe how small this town is? In walks Lauren and she's staying here."

"A small town," he murmured as he skimmed off his cap, sending a fine shower of snow flying.

"I need to get downstairs. Rick's trying to tinker with the boiler. I was helping him, then got sidetracked." She patted Lauren on the arm. "Thanks for being such a good sport." She turned to Duncan. "Thanks for the trip to Las Vegas. I had a great time."

She headed down the stairs, and Lauren looked back at Duncan. Why had Annie gone to Las Vegas without her husband? It didn't make sense. "Were you lucky in Las Vegas?" she asked Duncan.

"Actually, I hit the jackpot."

"Annie must have loved that."

"Annie was with her sister while I took care of some business," he said. "We're friends. She needed a ride, and I was going her way."

"Oh," she said. He kept looking at her. "What?"

"Oh, I was just thinking that first we meet on the

road, then at Rusty's and now here, at this time of night." He flicked his eyes over her from head to toe, then back to her face again.

She felt heat in her cheeks. "Small town," she said, echoing his words.

As Duncan slowly began to undo his jacket, he said, "If I didn't know better, I'd say you were stalking me."

She knew the best defense was a good offense, so she went for the offense. "Or maybe you're stalking me," she countered. "You're the one who almost ran into my car."

He looked at her for a long moment, then suddenly smiled. "Either way, here we are."

She had seen a faint version of the smile before, but now his whole face altered. He looked younger and… She bit her lip. Damn sexy. The way he was looking at her, and the way his voice lowered as he spoke, made her stomach tighten. He was flirting with her? That cold, distant person she'd seen up to now was starting to shift right in front of her eyes. "There's a lot of people in this very place," she said, her voice sounding a bit unsteady.

That smile lingered and so did its effect on her. "Not right now," he murmured. "It's just you and me."

"Since it's after midnight," she said quickly, "I wouldn't expect a crowd." She wanted to cut this conversation off right now. "Now, I need to get to bed. I have to change rooms in the morning."

"What?"

This was easy to explain. "It seems that some couple rents the room every ski season, but this year they're getting a divorce and with no snow, Annie thought they wouldn't be back. But it snowed and, for some reason, the man wants the room. So I get to move."

He shrugged. "There are some nice places in town."

"Like the one that buys snow in July?"

She regretted speaking without thinking, because the smile came back, playing at the corners of his mouth again. "That's one of them," he murmured.

"Well, I can't afford that kind of place, and I like it here. Besides, my car's not terribly dependable, and in this cold weather, I'm not sure how it's going to act, so I need to be able to walk to work."

"I thought you said you had to leave?"

"Annie has a room upstairs, an old chambermaid's room, actually, and she's letting me move in there."

The smile was gone. "The cubbyhole in the dormer?"

"That's the one, and it's all I need," she said and shifted nervously, more and more aware of the way she looked and the fact that she was naked under her robe. "Now, I'm tired." She didn't bother stifling a yawn. "I need to get to sleep. It's awfully late."

He hesitated, then checked his watch. When he looked back at her she thought she must have been imagining him flirting with her before. That cold distance was back full force. "It is late," he said, then turned and said "Good night" over his shoulder and went to his room, unlocked the door and went inside.

"Good night," she said softly, then turned to go back into her own room.

She closed her door, then headed to the bathroom and

turned on the water again. She took a quick shower, put on an oversize T-shirt her brother had given her from his school in Arizona, then turned off the lights and climbed into the old sleigh bed. She settled back into the softness that held the faint fragrance of lavender and tried to relax. She needed to get a good night's sleep. She had a lot to do tomorrow.

She rolled onto her side, closed her eyes and exhaled. After her reaction to his smile and her stupid idea he was flirting, getting closer without getting herself into some sort of awkward situation was going to be a challenge. She bit her lip, remembering when he'd smiled and her reaction to it. But her attraction to him was her problem, she thought, not his.

Lauren heard a door open and close downstairs, then she rolled over, snuggling under the covers with a sigh. A few moments later, she heard a muffled thump in the hallway near her door then a soft knocking sound. She sat up, uncertain whether the knock had been on her door. Then she heard it again, and knew it wasn't her door. The knock was next door at Duncan's room. She got out of bed and crossed to the door, slowly easing it open just enough to peek into the hallway.

In the dim light, she could just make out the back of someone standing by Duncan's door. The figure wore a bulky dark jacket with a collar pulled high, leggings and chunky boots, all covered with snow. The person moved from foot to foot until the door opened.

"I didn't think you'd come," she heard Duncan say in a low voice.

"You don't know how lucky you are." It was a soft,

feminine whisper, then the woman disappeared into Duncan's room.

Duncan's door closed with a quiet click and all that was left in the hallway were puddles of moisture from where the visitor had stood. Lauren stepped back into her room, closed the door quietly and stood very still in the darkness.

There was a muffled sound next door, and instinctively Lauren closed her eyes. As she listened, Lauren had an odd sensation in her stomach. She heard a low murmur, soft and almost unintelligible, but definitely a woman's voice. Then a deeper voice. Duncan's. She had images of the P.I.s in old movies getting a water glass and pressing it to the wall to listen in on what was going on next door.

But all she did was stand there, straining to make out what they were saying. There was a thumping sound, near the wall that separated the rooms. Another thump, but not as sharp as the last one. Another sound, softer, more distant, then more voices. She didn't know why each sound made her stomach knot so painfully, but after standing there in the dark for several minutes, she hurried back to her bed. She pulled the covers up to her chin and lay on her back staring at the ceiling. A small noise, another, a thump again, then voices murmuring, more rustling.

Lauren rolled onto her side and pulled her knees up to her chest. She'd thought, for a short while, that Duncan was with Annie. But she'd been wrong. Now there was this other woman who visited Duncan's hotel room after midnight.

Lauren had spent a lot of time trying to figure out why he'd left L.A., why he'd broken off his relationship with his father and with Bishop International. She'd come up with anger, stupidity, ego, maybe even the first volley in a fight against his father for control of the empire. But once she'd learned that Adrianna Barr was still in L.A. and had no contact with him, she hadn't thought of a woman being at the core of his actions.

Another thump sounded and she found herself grabbing a pillow and pulling it over her head. Then again, maybe he was what his father had told her, a man who wouldn't be without a woman, and, goodness knows, any woman would look at Duncan Bishop more than once, even if he worked at a diner in a resort town. She kept the pillow over her head, stretched her legs out, breathed evenly and felt herself drifting off to sleep.

Lauren woke suddenly to a loud sound. At first she thought it came from Duncan's room, but then realized it was a rumbling sound, growing to a crescendo and coming from outside. The sound faded and she glanced at the clock on the nightstand. Six o'clock.

She scrambled out of bed with just a half hour to get to work. She started to the bathroom, but glanced at the window and crossed to it. Pulling back the delicate material Lauren looked down on the main street of a transformed Silver Creek.

The small town had come to life, with cars and people everywhere. What was once a peaceful street was now hurried and bustling. And snow covered everything. She blinked at the stark whiteness, and the rumbling sound came back. She saw a huge snowplow coming from the north, lumbering down the street, shoving what looked like at least a foot of snow to the sides, piling it against the parked cars. People strolled up and down the wooden walkways, pushing through the piled snow to dart across the street between the cars making their way north.

Silver Creek was alive, and she could almost feel the energy that a foot of newly fallen snow had brought with it. She went into the bathroom, took a quick shower, dressed in jeans, a loose navy sweater and her running shoes. She ran a comb through her hair, grabbed her jacket and left her room.

She looked at Duncan's closed door, paused just a second to listen and didn't hear a thing. Not a sound. Either they were still sleeping or they'd left. She hurried down the stairs to the lobby and was at the door before she heard Annie call out, "Lauren, good morning!"

Lauren stopped and glanced back at the front desk. Annie was behind the counter, placing mail in the old-fashioned mail sorter that hung behind the desk. She looked almost painfully bright and cheerful, emphasized by the true pink of her long-sleeved shirt and a matching headband in her hair.

"Breakfast is ready," she said.

"No, thanks, I slept late and have to get to work."

"Oh, honey, you should have left a wake-up call."

"I wish I'd thought of it," she said as she grabbed the door latch.

"I meant to get you a key to the third-floor room so you could move your things. It's my fault, so I'll do what I told you I'd do. You'll be all moved up there when you get back."

Lauren stopped and grimaced. She'd totally forgotten about changing rooms today. "I'm sorry. I meant to move this morning."

"Well, I forgot the key. So I'll take care of things. And I've got some muffins back there if you'd like one to get you going?"

Lauren had all of her notes and files in a box in the trunk of her car, so there was nothing in her room but her clothes and toiletries. "No, thanks, I'm late."

Annie straightened and picked up the remaining envelopes. "Oh, I forgot to tell you, I'll make an adjustment on your room rate."

"Thanks so much," Lauren said and hurried outside, flipping her parka up over her hair as the frigid air hit her full force. She had forgotten to put on her snow boots but didn't have time to go back and change. So she made the best of it, carefully stepping in existing footsteps on the snowy walkway. Thankfully, someone had cut a path through the piled snow between the parked cars, to give access to the street, so she could cross. By the time she stepped into the diner, her face almost felt numb from the cold.

She stopped just inside the door, inhaling the mingled fragrances of cooking bacon, coffee and toast, and saw Rusty behind the counter.

"'Morning," Rusty called to her. "Put your things away, then get on out here," he said. "The day's started."

She hung her jacket in the office, grabbed her apron

and headed back to the dining room. Rusty told her which section she'd be handling and she got to work.

Duncan was nowhere to be seen, but she was too busy to dwell on his whereabouts. For the rest of the day, Lauren barely took a breath. People came in and out in droves, mostly for hot drinks, chili or stew, and to warm up before heading out into the snow and cold again. Still, by the afternoon, there was no sign of Duncan.

It was close to three when Rusty asked, "How you holding up?"

She exhaled. "I never knew so many people could drink so much coffee and hot chocolate."

Rusty grinned. "Yeah, they can go through both pretty quick, that's for sure. Can you work tomorrow morning, same hours?"

"Sure. I'll be here at six-thirty," she said and glanced at the clock. She had ten minutes left of her shift.

As though he'd read her mind, Rusty said, "Why don't you head on home? It's slow for now, and we can handle things."

She wasn't going to argue, but she sure wanted to find Duncan. "I thought Duncan would be here today since it's so busy," she said.

"Oh, no, he took off. He does that pretty often."

"Where does he go?" she asked, taking off her apron.

"No idea. One time he said he had something personal to take care of, but that's about as specific as he gets. He always tells me when he's leaving, just not why or where he's going. He said he'd be back tonight or tomorrow morning."

She could guess what he was doing, or at least who he was doing it with, but not where he was doing it. "Well, I'll be going," she said.

"I'll put that away for you," Rusty said, motioning to her apron. "You go and get some rest."

"Thanks." She headed to the office to get her jacket, and a few minutes later stepped out into the frigid afternoon. She pulled the hood on her jacket up over her head, nestled her chin in the collar and plunged her hands into her pockets. Heading toward the hotel, Lauren passed people as they wandered along the street, window-shopped, sipped hot drinks and laughed. Cars mostly made their way north, and there was piped music coming from hidden speakers near the walkway, giving a background of Christmas music that fit perfectly with the snow.

She'd basically wasted a day in Silver Creek. No Duncan. No way to make any sort of connection to get the job done. She didn't know if he'd left town, maybe gone back to Las Vegas, or if he was with the woman from the night before. Maybe he and the woman left town and were staying in a more private bed-and-breakfast.

It was unsettling that she found the very idea of him being with a stranger so distasteful. "He's a man who likes women," D.R. had said. And it seemed that was the case. Heck, one smile and he had her thinking things she had no right to think. She realized it was snowing again. The sky had turned leaden and heavy with clouds.

She walked slowly and as though the very thought of him had conjured him up, she spotted Duncan way down the street, coming toward her. His watch cap was pulled low, his head down, his heavy jacket straining across his broad shoulders. He walked quickly, then suddenly veered off between two cars, stepped out onto the road at a break in the traffic and strode quickly across to the other side. She cut between cars herself, ignoring the snow seeping into her running shoes to hurry after him.

He'd stopped on the walkway in front of a silver-jewelry store, a woman by his side. She couldn't make out the woman's face, but she could see she was in fur from head to foot. She was tall and thin, even in the shapeless clothes, and was looking up at Duncan. Then she stood on tiptoes and kissed him quickly.

Lauren saw an opening in the traffic and stepped out into the street. Just then, Duncan turned, lifting his face to look up at the darkening sky. Lauren stopped dead in her tracks. It wasn't Duncan. She'd been fooled by his size and the jacket he was wearing with a black watch cap. At the same moment she realized her mistake, she heard the blare of a horn, turned and saw a huge red car skidding toward her.

Chapter Six

Duncan had spotted Lauren when she left the diner and had followed her movements. Luckily he was there when the red car had trouble stopping. Acting on instinct, he rushed toward her, caught a handful of her jacket and jerked her back with all his strength. Together they tumbled backward, out of harm's way. Lauren landed against him and he put his arms around her. One look and his heart lurched in his chest. The red car had come to a stop less than a foot from them, on the spot where Lauren had stood. He held her tightly, took a moment to take air into his lungs, then stood up with her still in his arms.

"Good God," he whispered against her hair.

The passenger window of the car that had nearly hit her was rolled down and a florid-faced man in his mid-fifties screamed, "Is she crazy or what? She stopped right in front of me!"

"Move it," Duncan yelled at the man, then realized that Lauren was shaking. No, they were both shaking.

The car took off and it shocked him that he was holding on to Lauren so tightly. He eased his hold, shifting to put his hands on her shoulders. He couldn't make himself let go of her completely. She stared up at him with those lavender eyes, and he could feel the unsteadiness still in her. "Are you okay?" he breathed.

Her eyes closed for a moment, then her tongue touched her lips. He had to force his hold on her to stay light and not pull her back against him. She exhaled a heavy sigh. "I think so. I...I just saw the car, then you..." She bit her lip and trembled.

He was used to thinking clearly and acting on instinct. But in that moment, he wasn't thinking clearly, unable to rid his mind of that image of her in the road and the car heading right for her. Reason had no place in his actions, just instinct and maybe fear. His feelings were all blurred and jumbled when he bent over her and found her trembling lips with his.

The only thing he knew for sure was he had to kiss her. He had to make that contact, to have that connection, to feel her heat. And he did. Just for a moment, a flash in time, then he drew back and looked down at her. Her rich, dark hair emphasized the paleness of her skin, and the deep lavender of her eyes showed the same shock he felt.

Duncan stepped back, letting her go, pushing his hands in the pockets of his jacket. He'd had no right to kiss her. None. Not even to reassure himself that she was okay. "You could have been killed," he muttered, mounting tension in every word.

The world went on around them, cars going by, people barely sparing them a glance, and she didn't move for a very long moment. Then she suddenly hugged her arms around herself and stammered, "You—I—I didn't see the car."

"Why did you stop right in the middle of the road?"

She shrugged, looking away from him, and he didn't miss the way she gingerly touched her mouth before putting her hands in her pockets. "I was… I got distracted," she said, turning from him to look up and down the street. "I thought… I was wrong. I…shouldn't have done that."

She almost jumped out of her skin when a man came off the walkway, speaking in a loud voice. "Are you two moving or what?"

Duncan looked at the thin, balding guy in a tie-dyed ski jacket. "What?" he asked.

"I need to get out," he said, motioning to the parked car to Duncan's left. "You're in my way."

Lauren moved, bumping into Duncan, and he had her by the arm before he had time to think about touching her again. He felt her stiffen slightly, but she didn't pull away from him. "Let's get you to the hotel," he murmured and looked up and down the street to check the traffic. He didn't wait for her response before he drew her with him into the street and across to the other side.

He let go of her as they headed for the hotel, and he didn't look at her until they'd reached the entrance. Then he glanced at her, and she stepped past him. He watched her reach for the door, push it back and step into the lobby. He went after her. The space was empty, but he could hear voices coming from the room behind the registration desk.

Lauren turned to him. She was still pale, but high

color dotted her cheeks now. He didn't miss the way she clasped her hands tightly in front of her. "Thank you," she said. "I can't tell you how—"

He moved closer to her, letting himself touch her lips with the tip of his forefinger. Heat and silk. The sensation jolted through him. "I was there and you're okay." He drew back, pushing his hand behind him. "That's all that counts."

"Hey, you two," Annie called as she came through the curtained doorway behind the counter. Her smile faltered when she approached them. "Is something wrong?"

Lauren never looked away from him. "I almost got hit by a car." She said the words flatly. "Duncan saved my life."

Annie looked from one to the other. "What?"

Still Lauren didn't look away. "He pulled me back before the car could hit me."

Annie was smiling at him. "You saved her life, Duncan." She grabbed him by the arm. "My gosh, that's fantastic!"

He didn't want accolades from Annie. He just wanted… He looked at Lauren and he knew what he wanted—to spend time with her. To talk to her, and figure out why it seemed so important to him to do that very thing. "I saved your life, and you know what that means, don't you?" he asked as he undid his jacket and slipped it off.

"I'm grateful to you?" she said, looking vaguely uncertain.

He threw his jacket over his shoulder, hooking the

collar in one finger. "You obviously don't know about the rules, do you?"

She frowned slightly. "Rules?"

"When someone saves your life. The rules."

She frowned slightly. "I don't know what you're talking about."

"If you save someone's life, you're responsible for that person forever. And I saved your life."

The color in her cheeks was darkening a bit, and her look was solemn now. "I never heard that rule."

Annie cut in. "I have. You save a life, you're responsible for that life. Although I'm not sure it's forever."

Duncan liked Annie, but wished she had something else to do besides stand there listening to them. "It's for a long time," he said, never taking his eyes off of Lauren.

He'd hoped for a smile, some gentle teasing, anything but her staring at him with what bordered on anxiety. "Isn't there any way out of it?" she asked.

He glanced at her lips, searching for any hint of a smile, but instead all that did was remind him that her taste was probably still on his own lips. "I think the only way out is if the person you saved saves you right back." He shrugged. "I don't intend to step out in front of a car anytime soon, but why don't we figure something out." Although this had started as a game, a way to get around to asking her out, now everything had shifted. He wanted to spend more time with her, and he wanted her to want that, too. "What if I let you buy me dinner? Don't you think that would make us even?"

For some reason the color in her cheeks deepened slightly. "I don't know."

Annie continued to stand there, looking from one to the other, and then she nudged Lauren. "Take him up on it."

"Sure, take me up on it," he said, ready for a break. He'd had a hell of a day until Adrianna's sudden appearance. The quick meeting when he hadn't expected it, her coming out of a shop and running right into him, her current woes with a Swiss ski champion, her insisting on talking to him, and then showing up at his room last night.

"You have things to do," she said.

He'd planned on moving sooner or later, even if Adrianna hadn't shown up, but he wasn't ready to leave Silver Creek just yet. He looked down at Lauren and he knew that meeting her had made him even more reluctant to move on. Adrianna was gone in search of her boyfriend with the promise that she wouldn't talk to D.R. He didn't trust her, but he knew for now she was going to be tied up with her own life. "I had some personal things to take care of. But I'm done."

For some reason his words made her expression tighten. He didn't understand why. Any more than he understood why she was the kind of woman who could take his breath away. "Well, I've got things to do myself," she said abruptly. With that, she ducked around him, and he watched as she took the stairs two at a time. He didn't understand what had just happened. They'd been flirting, at least he had been, then she'd literally cut him off and left.

It wasn't about his ego. He didn't expect women to fall all over him. But her reaction bothered him. That and the fact that last night, when he'd finally gotten rid of Adrianna and fallen asleep, it was Lauren who had appeared in his dreams. He wasn't sure how or what happened in the dreams, but when he'd awakened, he'd been tied in knots and more than ready to get out of the hotel. If he was being realistic, he knew that he wasn't in any position to get involved with anyone right now. But that didn't stop the fantasies, or the frustration.

He looked at Annie, who was smiling at him with a touch of mischievousness. "Now this is getting interesting."

"Excuse me?"

"First your midnight visitor, and a beauty, I might add. Now Lauren. It's all very…well…interesting." She tapped him on the chest. "I hope you know how to juggle and do it well."

Duncan knew that Annie was a mother hen. She and her husband had never had children, so she tended to make her guests her "kids." But he didn't want her meddling like this. "There is no juggling act," he said. "The woman last night was a friend, that's all, and Lauren works at Rusty's."

Thankfully, she backed down. "Okay, friend, co-worker. Works for me," she said.

"Annie?"

He turned at the sound of Lauren's voice and saw her on the stairs. She wasn't looking at him. "I don't have a key for the new room," she said.

"Oh, shoot," Annie said and hurried back to the desk. "I forgot. Sorry." She reached across the desk and grabbed a key off the hooks on the wall. "I got sidetracked." She crossed to where Lauren stood and handed her the key. "Your things are in the room, and I left extra towels and a blanket on the bed. Just let me know if you need anything else, okay?"

"Thanks," Lauren said, then darted a quick look to Duncan. "I was thinking about what you said, and maybe we could have coffee or something, in a little while?"

Or something? "Sure," he said. "When?"

She glanced at the wall clock by the entry door, then back at him. "How about in an hour? I'll meet you at the coffee shop across from Rusty's."

"You got it," he said, then she turned and went back upstairs and out of sight.

Annie cleared her throat, and when he looked at her, she winked, then headed back into the downstairs living area she shared with her husband. Coffee? He'd settle for that. Maybe get to know her a bit better and figure out what, if anything, he wanted with her.

Duncan headed upstairs to his room, went inside and tossed his jacket on the bed that faced the windows. The room was larger than most, with its own bath, decorated in every shade of blue known to man, mixed with cherry-wood and mahogany antiques. He'd chosen it because it had the largest bed in the hotel, a king-size mahogany sleigh bed that was roomy enough for his long frame.

He stripped off his clothes, turned on the water in the shower stall and headed to the phone. After two rings his call was answered. "The Inn at Silver Creek. How may I direct your call?"

"Adrianna Barr?"

"I'm sorry, sir, Ms. Barr checked out this afternoon."

He hung up, satisfied that Adrianna was finally gone. And that was that. He'd realized last night that there was nothing between them. And all he asked of her was not to tell D.R. where she'd seen him. She was so obsessed with her skier he hoped talking to D.R. wasn't even a thought. He exhaled, then went back into the bathroom and stepped into the shower.

Reaching for the soap, he lifted his face to the warmth of the spray and lathered his body. From nowhere came a flashing memory of snatching Lauren out of the path of the car, then holding her. Despite the bulky jackets, he'd felt her slender body against his, the trembling that was a result of shock, then the kiss. The images started affecting his body.

He tried to shut them off, but they seeped into his mind. The images, the sensations, her taste. So potent that they made his body start to ache. He scrubbed his body harder, then gave up. And when he gave up, he realized that the fantasies were less about sex, and maybe more about not being alone. "Damn it," he said angrily. "Damn it."

No woman should be able to make him feel this isolated simply by not being there. Or make him realize that he'd been isolated all his life. He reached for the faucet and, with a sharp twist, turned the water from hot to cold. Very cold.

LAUREN GOT TO THE COFFEE SHOP first, cradled her mug in her hands and watched for Duncan from the small table by the windows. He was nowhere in sight. She checked the wall clock in the tiny, rustic shop—five minutes late.

She sat back in the wooden chair, loosening her jacket, then slipping it off of her shoulders and onto the upright back of the chair. She tugged at the cuffs of her blue sweater, then nervously combed her hair with her fingers. She'd panicked when he'd suggested dinner. The kiss had unnerved her almost as much as the incident with the car. She'd tried to forget about both things, and concentrate on how she'd handle this time with him.

She looked out the window again. Still no Duncan. She fingered her mug and shook her head when the waitress offered a refill. Just as she was ready to get up and leave, she saw him. He strode down the street like a man on a mission. He looked neither right nor left, head down, walking straight and letting people move out of his way. When he entered the coffee shop he spotted her immediately.

She wasn't sure what she'd expected him to do or say when he arrived, but it certainly wasn't that he'd say, "Let's go," then wait for her to do as he said.

She didn't move. "You just got here."

He frowned. "We need to leave. There's another place farther down the road."

She wanted to argue, and not go anywhere with Duncan, but she ended up standing and reaching for her jacket. When she started to put it on, Duncan helped her, tugging it up over her arms then shoulders. As they exited he placed his hand at the small of her back. She didn't know what was going on, but she could feel tension in his touch and a sense of urgency.

Once they were outside, Duncan walked beside her and

didn't touch her. He walked quickly and she tried to keep up. Finally, she just stopped and it took him two strides to realize she wasn't beside him any longer. He turned, came back to her and said in a low voice, "What's wrong?"

"Tell me where we're going."

"For coffee."

"I had coffee."

"For more coffee."

"What's going on?" she asked, deciding that there, on the busy street, was as good a place as any to call him on his behavior.

He exhaled. "Nothing, I just thought another place would be better."

"No."

"What?" he asked with a frown.

"No, that's not it. Tell me the truth, or I'll go back to the hotel and act as if this never happened, and it never will happen again."

She was bluffing. But she had to understand why he was doing what he was doing before she went any farther. "Why are you being so difficult?" he asked, leaning closer to her.

"Me? You're the one who dragged me out of the perfectly nice coffee shop and away from my drink."

He exhaled, pushing his hands in the pockets of his jacket. "Okay, okay," he muttered, then looked around. "Over there," he said, and nodded with his head to what looked like a small grocery store.

She hesitated, then agreed. "Okay."

They went across the street, side by side but not touching, and stepped into what she'd thought was a grocery store. Part of it contained groceries, but the other part was divided into something labeled Cinnamon World. Duncan walked with her over to what turned out to be another coffee shop, one filled with the overwhelming smell of cinnamon—buns, cakes, doughnuts.

Duncan steered her toward the nearest table, then crossed to the counter, ordered two coffees and finally came back with a mug in each hand. As they sat, sipping their coffee, Lauren waited for him to speak. Just when her nerves were starting to fray, he looked up at her with his dark eyes. "I guess that all looked strange, didn't it?"

"I'd say so," she said, cupping the warm mug between her hands. "Pretty darn strange."

He took his time undoing his jacket, but he didn't take it off. Instead, he drank more coffee, and she waited again, ignoring her coffee completely. He finally sat back, his mug on the table, his hands resting on either side of it. "I didn't want to be in that place right then," he finally said. "I wanted to be someplace else."

One thing her boss, Vern, had taught Lauren was, when you were trying to get information, let the other person talk. People obsessively filled in empty spaces, as if they couldn't stand a void in conversation. Silence bothered people and they did all they could to fill it. They'd talk to hear themselves talk and, usually, they gave something away. So she waited without saying anything.

He cocked his head to one side and said, "You're good."

"What?"

"You're good. You aren't the kind of woman who talks and talks and talks. You sit and look at me with those eyes, and let me talk." He smiled slightly. "You are definitely no Annie."

She smiled. "I like Annie." And she did.

"I do, too, but…" He shrugged. "She's…I don't know."

"I know. She's either the nicest, most friendly upbeat person you ever met, or she's the most annoying person."

He sat forward, his smile growing. "As I said, you're good."

"And you're not off the hook with that compliment. Why did you do all that outside?"

He chuckled softly. "Okay, okay," he murmured, then deliberately took another sip before saying, "I saw someone I didn't want to run into. It's that simple."

"Who?"

"Just someone I thought had left town."

She decided to just say what was on her mind, get it out in the open and see how he reacted. "The woman in your room last night?"

Bingo. Bull's-eye. His expression tightened, then he exhaled roughly as he sat forward. "What do you know about that?"

She shrugged. "I heard her at your door, then saw her go in." She reached for her mug, just to hold on to something. "I figured if you were having coffee with me, the last person you'd want to see would be a woman you spent the night with."

She hated the words as she said them, but she didn't take them back. She watched Duncan, waiting for the shift in his gaze, that discomfort that she knew would come, then maybe some lies, something to cover up what had happened. "I wasn't with her last night, first of all. She was there half an hour, tops." She knew she looked skeptical, but she didn't care. "We were talking and figuring things out."

She waited.

"She's someone I knew before, someone I dated. That's true, but it's been over for a long time."

"Then why didn't you want her to see you with me?"

He nodded. "Good question."

She didn't want a critique, she wanted answers. "Why?"

"Because, she's…" He pushed his coffee away. "Okay, let me just put this bluntly. We broke up. We went on with our lives, and now she's in a bind with her new boyfriend and she wants me to—" he shrugged sharply "—God, I don't know what she wants."

It had been Adrianna Barr. Lauren was certain. That's who had gone to his room last night. "What do you want?"

He looked right at her. "Not her. Not now."

"Are you sure? No second thoughts?"

He looked right at her. "Very sure, and no second thoughts."

He said the words simply and without blinking. Unless he was a terrific liar, he was telling her the truth. "So, you're hiding from her?"

Duncan smiled and a dimple appeared to the left of his mouth. "No, I just don't have the time for dealing with Adrianna right now. Besides, I have other things I want to do."

"What things?" she asked.

"Getting to know you better."

Chapter Seven

The words hung between them, and Lauren felt as if she'd gone into a whirlwind that had started with the kiss. She had to get out of it. Right away. So she said the first thing she could think of to stop it. "I'm sorry, but I'm not looking for a relationship."

He studied her for a long moment, then finally said, "Okay, that's honest enough." Then he drank the last of his coffee and put the mug back onto the table. "Ready to go?"

She didn't want him to just cut her off like that. She couldn't have a relationship with him, but she had to make this work because of her job. "I didn't mean to be rude or offend you," she said.

"You weren't and you didn't," he said. "I'm the one who read things wrong." He stood. "It's not the first time I've done that," he said. "And it won't be the last."

He motioned to her coffee. "Do you want to take it with you?"

She looked down at the cup. "No, thanks," she said and stood.

Together they stepped out into the cold late afternoon and silently headed back to their hotel. Lauren couldn't figure out what to say. She didn't want to cut off everything between them, just the dangerous things.

"Are you working tomorrow?" she finally asked.

"I've got things to do" was all he said and didn't stop walking.

Okay, he might or might not show up at the diner tomorrow. "Are you going to see Adrianna?" she asked, figuring things couldn't get much worse than they were right then.

"No." Nothing else.

She'd blown it. She walked in silence by his side, past Rusty's, farther up, and they reached the spot where she'd almost been hit earlier. They both veered toward the road, and surprisingly Duncan reached out to take her hand. He stopped beside her, between the cars, and said, "Just making sure we get across safely."

She felt his fingers curl around hers and she found herself doing the same thing, holding on to him while they waited for a break in traffic. Once it did, they crossed to the other side and the instant they hit the walkway, he let her go. She closed her hand in a light fist and hated the fact that she missed his hand around hers. She ducked her head into the snow that was falling harder now, and by the time they reached the hotel, she could barely look up without getting snow in her eyes.

Lauren pushed open the door, but Duncan remained outside. "You're not coming in?"

"Not right now," he said, then turned and walked off.

She closed the door, stomped on the scatter rug in the entry to rid her boots of clinging snow, then turned and saw an unfamiliar couple sitting by the windows at the front of the lobby. They glanced up and smiled, then went back to watching the street through the window. Thankfully, Annie wasn't anywhere in sight, and Lauren was able to escape to her room. She needed a couple PowerBars from her bag and a good night's sleep. In the morning she'd be able to figure out a plan of attack.

ALL PLANS WERE ON HOLD the next day since Duncan wasn't around. When she returned to the hotel, Duncan wasn't there, either. After grabbing a bite to eat, she went to her room and crawled into bed. She was failing this job miserably, and she hated that. Almost as much as not knowing where Duncan was or what he was doing.

Lauren fell asleep quickly for a change, but woke suddenly to total darkness, her heart racing and her skin damp with sweat. The car. Duncan. Kissing him. She fumbled for the light and got out of bed. She hated disturbing dreams, and she seldom had them. But this one had left her fighting for air and a need to get out of the small room. She looked at the clock on the bedside table. Eleven o'clock. She'd slept less than three hours.

Now that she was wide awake, she needed some fresh air. She quickly dressed in jeans, a T-shirt and her snow boots, then grabbed her jacket and headed downstairs to the second level. There was no light showing under Duncan's door, and the only sound was music drifting up from the lobby, a string version of "Silent Night." In the lobby, Lauren found a middle-aged man sitting on a side bench talking on a cell phone. He was dressed all in black, with a heavy gold necklace and a shaved head that gleamed in the light. He didn't seem to hear her at all.

"I told you, I'm here, and I'm having fun," he said into the phone. "It's not my fault—"

Lauren went outside, cutting off what she could hear of the man's conversation, and stopped on the single step. The snow had stopped, but not before putting a fresh curtain of white over everything. A few cars drove down the streets and a scattering of people were on foot. A couple, arm in arm, passed her without a glance, and more Christmas music drifted in the night from hidden speakers above the walkway.

She glanced at the glow of the ski slopes to the north, and closer, the twinkling Christmas lights that rimmed the windows of the closed shops. She hesitated, thought about going to get her car, but knew she needed to walk. She set off to the north, inhaling the clean, frigid air, and looked up at the sky. It was remarkably clear, with stars so brilliant she felt as though she could reach out and touch them.

Walking without a goal in mind, she took her time, sorting out her thoughts, looking in the windows of the closed shops. She stopped at a store that advertised old-time photographs. The displayed pictures were of people in costumes, obviously from the time of the silver strikes in the mid-1800s, from dance-hall girls to miners. And all were done in sepia tones.

She leaned closer to look at one and was startled when she sensed movement behind her.

"They always make it seem as if that period was so damn romantic," Duncan said.

She stared at his blurred reflection in the window and swallowed hard. It felt as though she'd been holding her breath until she saw him again. Stupid reaction, she reasoned, but so real she had to take a deep breath before she could speak. "You…you don't think it was romantic?" she asked without turning to face him. "That rugged determination, the uncertainty of everything, then striking the mother lode?"

"They don't get into the details, do they?"

"Such as?" she asked, preferring to talk to him like this, without having those dark eyes assessing her directly.

"Sickness, cold, misery, storms and empty claims. You name it," he murmured. "It was brutal."

"Well, you sound like the kind who looks at a glass as half-empty, instead of half-full."

He laughed softly. "It's called facing reality."

She turned then, and found herself facing her own reality. Duncan Bishop. But, thankfully, he was a man in the shadows. He'd stepped back far enough that the twinkling lights in the windows barely touched his features and only emphasized his size in the heavy jacket and boots. "I think it's called pessimism," she said.

He cocked his head slightly to his right. "You think?"

"You're losing the essence of the romance of that time period." She looked away from him, to glance back down the street into the old section. "You can almost imagine being thrown back in time here. Take away the cars and the electric lights and you'd have the old buildings and the ruggedness of the area with the mountains as a backdrop, and snow everywhere." She measured her next words carefully as she looked back at him. "Silver Creek would have been the kind of place when, if you were born here, even if you left, you'd be back. No matter what it took."

He stared at her hard, then asked, "Are you from a small town?"

She hadn't expected the question. "No, but home is home. I just thought around here, that's the way it would be done." She'd heard a few things today at work. "I heard that the guy who owns that exclusive resort up there, the inn, was born here. That his great-great something or other, maybe grandfather, was the founder of the town."

"And your point is?"

"He was born here, and I don't know if he left or not, but he's still here and doing well."

"I suppose that gives you the warm fuzzies?"

She blinked at him, and actually chuckled easily. "And I suppose it doesn't give you the warm fuzzies?"

Now it was his turn to laugh softly. "I can't remember when I last had a case of the warm fuzzies." He narrowed his eyes. "What are you doing out this late?"

She thought about lying, but decided that the truth would do just as well. "I couldn't sleep. That room is so darn small I had to get out and get some air. How about you?"

"I needed to get out, too."

"You've been gone awhile," she said. "Work's been crazy with the snow people flooding into town."

"I figured it would be busy" was all he said.

"It is, really busy."

He rocked forward slightly on the balls of his feet. "I don't want you to get the wrong idea, but I'm going up the street for a drink. Do you think you could come along and not feel as if you're being hit on?"

He was joking, making light of what she'd said earlier, but right then it was important for him to understand that she wasn't looking for any sort of entanglement. She couldn't afford that, period. "Maybe, but what if your ex walks in?"

"She won't," he said. "She's gone off with her skier to parts unknown."

"Is that why you've been gone? You've been getting her out of town?"

He shook his head. "No, I had personal things to do. Now, how about that drink?"

"I don't drink beer," she said, truthfully.

"Then have some coffee or tea or hot chocolate. I can't leave you out here alone, just wandering the streets. Besides, I need a drink."

"You *can't?*" she asked, arching one eyebrow.

"I told you all about the law that makes me responsible for you, well I'm taking that seriously. So come along with me, for protection purposes only, and we can get a drink."

"Where to?"

"Down the street, to a place called the Briar." He shifted from foot to foot. "Come on, I'm cold."

"Me, too."

He came closer, his voice low. She could see his eyes as black as the night. "Then come with me to get something to warm us."

She swallowed hard, intensely aware of his size and closeness. God, he was overwhelming. She had to force herself to concentrate on why she was here. "Okay, you talked me into it," she said and could hear a certain breathlessness in her tone. Damn it. "Which way?"

He took her by her shoulders, gently turning her to the north. "Straight ahead, three blocks, then left," he said.

"North it is." She moved ahead, breaking the contact, and took a deep breath of frigid air. It steadied her a bit, and as Duncan came up beside her, she had to adjust her pace to match the stride of his long legs.

"So, where are you from in Arizona?" he asked.

She almost missed her step at the question, but caught herself and kept going. "Excuse me?"

"Your car has Arizona plates on it. I was wondering where you came from."

She hadn't thought he'd noticed, but that was just why she'd used her brother's car, so nothing would connect her to the L.A. area and make Duncan suspicious. She thought she'd be the one putting out the questions, not being the recipient of them, but she could handle this. "My brother went to school there and he ended up living there. Since it's his car, it's got Arizona plates." All true.

But he wasn't satisfied and kept going. "Then where are you from, if you aren't from Arizona?"

She shrugged. "I've lived a lot of places." True again,

but she would not elaborate and tell him those "places" had all been around the Los Angeles area.

"West Coast?"

"Mostly."

"And no small towns?"

"Not that I remember," she said.

They passed a couple headed in the opposite direction and nodded, then continued on. And so did his questions. "So, you've got a brother?"

"Three of them."

"And where do you fall in the birth order?"

"Last. The kid sister." She had to get this talk back to him and away from her background. "I was the one who took all the ribbing and learned a few things about cars and such."

"Like getting a temperamental car going on a mountain road?"

"Exactly," she murmured. "How about you, any siblings?"

He touched her on the arm, but didn't answer the question. Instead, he said, "Turn here," and motioned her onto a side street, a quiet place where some cars were buried in snow by the curb. A group of older buildings lined the narrow street, then flowed into what looked like a semi-residential area beyond.

She saw a single sign that was still lit, a modest one compared to the ones on the main street. The Briar. It was located about a block off the main thoroughfare and from the outside, it didn't look like a place where people who knew Duncan Bishop would go. Adrianna wouldn't think to look here, she realized.

She was going to repeat her question about his siblings, knowing full well he was an only child. She wanted to get some information out of him, about himself, about his life, about his background so she could build on that. But before she could figure out how to word the question, they were at the bar.

The Briar was housed in a single-storied building, made of rough wooden and worn stone walls. Smoke curled out of a heavy chimney and high windows spilled light out into the night and onto the snow. They stopped by the entry, a heavy wooden door with an old-fashioned lantern hanging above it. Duncan reached past her to push back the door, and she felt his body along her back at the same time as she was hit by a wave of warmth from inside.

She quickly stepped up a single step and into the bar. A huge stone fireplace looked like it was part of the stone wall to the right, and tables were scattered around on the scarred wooden floor. A bar ran the length of the room to the left and two pool tables were clustered in the back. Christmas music played by a small dance area near an old-fashioned jukebox, and when they walked in the door, the customer count went up to seven.

A couple on the dance floor slowly moved to a mellow Christmas ballad, a man at the bar hovered over his half-empty beer mug and two men at the back were playing a game of pool. This was definitely not a place anyone would expect to find Duncan Bishop. He was beside her as she flipped off her hood, then touched her on the shoulder. "The bar or a table?"

"A table," she said, and headed for one near the

hearth. She felt his presence behind her, but she didn't look back. When she got to the table, he helped her remove her jacket. His hand brushed the exposed nape of her neck, and she jerked forward, freeing her arms from the sleeves. She turned and Duncan smiled, as though he, too, felt the jolt that went through her at his touch.

She hung her jacket over the back of the chair and sat down. Duncan had made his way to the jukebox and the fire. Lauren looked at the overhead beams laced with white twinkle lights that seemed to be everywhere in Silver Creek, then at the bar and the smoky mirror behind it. When Duncan touched her hand, it startled her. She looked at him, drawing her hand back at the same time. "What?"

"What do you want to drink?" he asked, drawing his hand back to press it flat against the wooden tabletop.

In that moment, she realized how very different he and his father really were. D.R. was a cold, controlling man, almost indifferent to the presence of others, and beyond handshakes, with no need to touch anyone. But Duncan seemed to make physical connections without thinking about it. A touch to get her attention, to guide her inside, to show her the way to go. Touching. Always touching.

He started to say, "I asked you—" but never got to finish because the bartender arrived and set down a dish of pretzels on the table between them.

The man was middle-aged, rail thin, with slicked-back hair, dressed all in black. He nodded to Duncan. "Evening, Duncan," he said. "The usual?"

"Yeah, draft," Duncan said, then the bartender looked at Lauren and smiled.

"Draft for you, too, honey?"

Alcohol was really out of the question, even if she liked beer. Which she didn't. She didn't need to have her thinking blurred any more than it was right now. "I don't like beer," she said.

"Well, honey, what about some wine? Got white, red, blush?" When she shook her head, he said, "I have the perfect drink for you, my holiday punch made with imported strawberries. It's a thing of beauty."

She could do punch. "Okay, that sounds good."

He nodded. "By the way, I'm Pudge."

"Lauren."

"Well, Lauren, I'll get you that drink," he said and took off to the bar.

She waited until he was out of earshot, then asked Duncan, "Pudge, as in being pudgy?"

He shrugged. "I never asked." A song started on the jukebox, a Christmas song that was smooth and slow, and without warning, Duncan sat forward and said, "Do you dance?"

She couldn't drink around him, and she surely couldn't dance with him. "Not really," she said, and looked around, then asked, "Do you play pool?"

"Don't tell me you're a pool shark?" he asked, skimming off his knit cap and stuffing it in the pocket of his jacket.

"I do okay. My brothers played, and I learned by osmosis."

Duncan stood, stripped off his jacket and tossed it over the back of his chair. "Come on. Let's see how good you picked it up by osmosis."

"You've got it," she said, getting up and heading back toward the empty pool table. She could play pool. She couldn't let him close enough to dance. It was that simple. She crossed to the rack and picked out a cue stick. Duncan did the same. "So, what's the bet going to be?" he asked.

"Well, I'm broke, so money's out," she said, concentrating on the color of the T-shirt he was wearing with jeans, a simple gray cotton that molded to his chest. "What did you have in mind?"

His eyes flicked down to her lips, then back to her eyes. "I'll think about it," he murmured.

Damn, damn, damn, she thought. It was there again, that flirty teasing they seemed to slip into so easily. Getting to know him was one thing, but there was that unspoken thing between them, that possibility of something more. "We have to know before we start," she said. "We have to know what's at stake." She sure needed to know.

"Okay, the loser has to take the winner's muffin that Annie insists on giving everyone for breakfast. And, they have to eat it."

"A muffin?"

"Oh," he said, reaching to get a piece of chalk and rubbing the end of his pool cue as his dark eyes held hers. "You haven't had the muffins yet, have you?"

"No, I didn't have time the first morning and I haven't seen Annie the past couple mornings."

He grinned and the dimple was there. "This gets better and better. Annie is a great person, kind, welcoming, looks out for every need you have. But, and this is the biggie, she can't bake. Oh, she thinks she can, and everyone humors her, but she makes these horrendous bran muffins and insists you have one every morning." He leaned closer to her, so close that she felt his breath on her skin when he said, "Between you and me, I have a few hidden in my room hardening into doorstops."

She smiled. "You're kidding."

"No, I'm not." He drew back, a smile of his own echoing hers. "So, is it a bet?"

"Do the muffins *have* to be eaten?"

"I think that should be part of it, don't you?"

She could do this. Eating an inedible muffin was a breeze compared to... She felt her stomach tighten. What had she thought he'd want to bet? And why was she so darn relieved it was just a muffin?

When Duncan drew back, muffins were the last thing on his mind. What he'd really wanted would guarantee she'd run in the opposite direction. But one good thing Duncan had learned from his father was the importance of appearing patient, even when you weren't. Especially if what you wanted was worth the time and effort to get it. He had a feeling that Lauren was worth whatever it took to get closer to her.

Duncan made himself move away, the raw knowledge that he wanted this woman tightening his middle. He wasn't quite sure when wanting a drink tonight had shifted to wanting to be with Lauren. Probably when he first saw her at the photographer's window. Probably when she looked at him in the reflection of the glass. Probably when he'd touched her shoulders. No, there was nothing probable about that. That was a definite.

Pudge brought over their drinks and placed them on a wall shelf by the cue rack. "They'll be safe there," he said and glanced at Lauren. "Haven't seen you around these parts before."

"I just got into town a few days ago," Lauren said.

"Oh, here for the skiing and…" He grinned. "The great ambiance?" He pronounced the word as *ambee-ants*.

"No, just going through and working for a while."

"You looking for a job?"

"She's got one, at Rusty's," Duncan said.

"Oh, you're the gal who's got that great old car?" Pudge asked.

"How did you know about my car?"

"Old Rollie's been salivating over it." Someone shouted over to him for a beer, and he waved to them, then said to Lauren, "Watch out for this guy, he's a real shark." With a wink, he went off to get the other man's order.

Duncan saw Lauren turn those eyes on him. "Oh, so you're the pool shark and you were accusing me of being one?"

"No," he said and was glad that he hadn't been able to sleep, that he'd gone out to get a drink because his room had seemed so vast and empty. He liked being here with her. "I beat Pudge three out of five games a week ago, and he hasn't forgiven me." He moved closer and realized he was trying to catch the soft scent that seemed to cling to her. "He's not that good, believe me, so I'm not that good, either."

She smiled at him, a gentle expression, and he

wished he could make her smile on command. "We'll see, won't we?" she murmured.

He guessed they would. One way or the other. He racked the balls, then looked at Lauren standing to his right, her drink untouched. "Rules?"

"Whatever you want."

"Okay, call shots?"

"You got it."

"Do you want to break?"

"You break," she said so softly he found himself staring at her lips. He looked away, quickly lined up his shot and broke the balls. A striped ball fell in the corner pocket, another one dropped into a side pocket.

"Stripes," he called and lined up his next shot. He really was a decent pool player. But as he drew back to take his next shot, he sensed Lauren behind him and as a result he missed his shot.

"Too bad," she murmured as she leaned halfway across the table, lined up her shot, called it and made it. Along with dropping two more balls with it. He got his beer, sipping the brew while she studied the table. Calling her next shot, she leaned forward and focused.

He couldn't take his eyes off of her. He just wanted to get to know her, he told himself. Wanted to know what made Lauren Carter tick. But he knew that he wanted so much more.

Chapter Eight

Duncan continued watching her line up shots, and make them. Lauren cast him quick looks, and he didn't miss the smile in her eyes with every move she pulled off.

They were at opposite ends of the table now, but her presence wasn't any less disturbing. God, he loved challenges, but he'd never before thought of a woman as a challenge. Until now.

"Okay," she said, smiled at him, and came around to reach for her drink.

He watched her take a sip as if tasting it to be sure she liked it, then she smiled again. "Boy, that's good." She took another drink, coughed softly, then put the mug down. She bent over the table again, studying the balls before walking around the table, getting closer to him. He found himself almost holding his breath as she got even closer to where he was standing.

This was ridiculous. He was thirty-eight years old, not some immature teenager. But he felt like one as she moved behind him and her body brushed his. He closed his eyes for a long moment, then opened them when she spoke to him. "Don't go to sleep. I need you to move."

He looked down at her, into those incredible eyes, then to her softly parted lips. No relationship. He could handle that part of it. No involvement. No, he wasn't going to let that stand. She repositioned her cue stick over and over again, and he took in the way she bent forward, the way the jeans strained against her hips, her long legs. He exhaled roughly, killing the thoughts that came so easily.

"Here goes nothing," she murmured, then tapped the cue ball, hit the closest ball and dropped it in the end pocket. The cue ball headed for the second ball, ticked it softly, but enough to send it toward the hole. It hit the lip of the pocket, seemed to hang there, then dropped in.

She turned to him, a huge smile on her face as she lifted her cue stick into the air. "Yes!"

"You've still got to drop the eight ball," Duncan said in a voice he knew sounded a bit too rough.

"First, a drink, then the victory." She reached for her mug, finished off the punch and motioned to Pudge for a refill. She licked her lips before setting down the empty mug. On her next shot she dropped the eight ball neatly, then turned to him, smiling. "Muffins, anyone?"

Damn, she was beautiful, Duncan thought.

"Got you, did she?" Pudge asked as he brought over Lauren's drink.

He shook his head. "Pudge, she's a ringer."

"Well, never trust a beautiful woman," the man said philosophically before heading back to the bar.

"Pool is just one more thing my brothers taught me. You know how it is with siblings? The old, 'you want to hang out with us, so you can't embarrass us,' and the next thing you know, you learn to play pool?"

He shrugged. "Actually, I don't."

"Don't tell me you're an only child?"

He reached for his beer again, then turned to her. "I think so, but with my father, you never know. He's full of surprises."

"You mean you could have a bother or sister somewhere out there and wouldn't know?"

He drained his beer before saying, "There's a possibility." He didn't know his father at all.

"Did your father play around a lot on your mother, or has he been married a ton of times?"

He'd worked with his father for years, been around him twenty hours a day at times, but he had trouble answering the first part of Lauren's question. His father never seemed to have time for much besides work. The man hardly had time for an affair before Duncan's mother died, but afterward, he could have had a hundred affairs and Duncan would never have known. "One marriage, and as to other woman, who knows?"

"He's still married to your mother?"

"No," he said and finished his beer completely. "She died ten years ago."

"Oh, I'm sorry," she said hoping she sounded sincere.

He brushed her off. "Let's sit at the table."

She lifted her cue stick in his direction. "Don't you want revenge?"

"I think I'll just get shot down again," he said.

"Hey, if you're too scared of me…"

Scared? No, he wasn't scared of her, but she asked questions he had little desire to think about, let alone answer. "Rack 'em up," he said.

She took a long drink before heading over to rack the balls. "Same bet?"

He nodded. "I've got muffins to spare."

Two games later, Lauren was undefeated, working on her fourth mug of punch, and Duncan was ready to leave. When he caught Pudge's eye for the bill, he realized that only one other customer was still in the bar. He turned to Lauren, who was putting her cue stick away, but as she reached toward the rack, the stick slid out of her hand and clattered to the floor.

Her eyes widened, then she dropped down to pick up the stick. Once she had it, Duncan watched as she sank farther and ended up sitting on the floor. Her legs were tucked under her and she sat there without moving, her eyes closed. When she didn't get up, he went over and hunkered down in front of her. "Lauren, are you okay?"

She opened her eyes at the sound of his voice and he realized the deep lavender gaze was slightly blurred. "I'm not sure," she whispered. "I don't know."

Pudge was there behind him. "What's going on?" he asked.

"I don't know. She bent down to get her cue stick, and—"

"What did she have, four cups of punch?"

"Four," she said. "It's…it's really tashty," she mumbled.

"You liked it?" Duncan asked.

She touched her tongue to her lips and the action ran

riot over his nerves. "Sure. It's really…really good, and shhhh…" Her tongue touched her lips quickly. "It was so fruity. Jush…jush…" She shook her head and enunciated with great care. "Just delicious."

Pudge chuckled as he stood over them. "I wondered how long it would take before that punch set in. She was drinking it like it was soda pop."

"What's in it?" Duncan asked.

"Fruit and stuff, and vodka. Everyone knows about my punch."

He didn't. He brushed back a tendril of Lauren's hair that clung to her cheek. Her skin was warm and soft under the tips of his fingers, and he had to force himself to pull his hand away and place it on his denim-clad thigh. "Lauren, you're drunk."

She frowned. "No, thash…that's jush fruit."

"Vodka," he said.

Her eyes widened as they lifted to look at the man standing over them. "You, you mean thash…thash…"

"Sorry, honey."

"Holy cow," she said quite clearly, and her head lolled back as she closed her eyes. The action started to tip her backward, and Duncan grabbed both her hands to keep her upright.

"It sneaks up on you, don't it?" Pudge asked.

"I'd say so," Duncan muttered, then slowly stood, pulling Lauren back to her feet. She wobbled, then got her balance, but she didn't let go of his hand as they made their way to their table. Pudge pulled out a chair and Duncan eased her down onto the hard wood. When he knew she was stable, he looked at Pudge. "Two coffees, strong."

"You bet," he said and took off.

Lauren exhaled and sat forward, burying her head in her hands. He thought she was saying "Damn it" over and over again, then she slowly lowered her hands and looked at him. "You knew?"

"No, I swear I didn't know. I don't drink punch of any kind, and I sure didn't know it was loaded with booze."

She exhaled again and combed her fingers through her rich hair, spiking it around her face. "I...it didn't taste bad, just sort of different and really warm when it went down. I never drink, really. I'm..." Her voice trailed off when Pudge came back with two steaming mugs of coffee, placing them down on the table.

Duncan watched her hands shake slightly as she reached for the mug.

Duncan took his and Pudge gave him a questioning look. "Anything else you might need?"

"Just the bill," he said.

"Forget it. This is on me," he said and strode off.

Duncan lifted his mug, sipped some of the startlingly strong coffee and watched Lauren over the rim. She was staring into the coffee mug. "I never..." She sighed. "Damn it. I don't." She looked distressed. She was drunk, and not because she'd tried to get drunk. She wasn't a loud drunk, or a violent drunk, or a mean drunk, at least not yet. But she looked totally distressed.

"Are you going to be sick?"

She moaned softly and barely shook her head. "No."

"Then drink some coffee and we'll get going to the hotel."

She cupped her mug and lifted it with both hands, sipped a bit of coffee and finally set it down with a soft thud. "I...I'm ready to go," she said.

"Are you sure?" he asked as she slowly stood and steadied herself, using the table to regain her balance.

"Yes, I...I'm sure. I need..." She turned slowly and reached for her jacket. Awkwardly, she pulled it off the chair and attempted to shove an arm in the sleeve. But all she succeeded in doing was spinning in a very slow circle.

Duncan got up and helped her slip on the jacket. He wasn't used to feeling this protective. He wanted to take care of Lauren. "Why don't I go back and get my car?" he asked. "You can wait here and have more coffee."

"No, I can walk," she said. She pressed one hand flat on the tabletop, then straightened and started across to the door.

"You have a good evening," Pudge called after her, but she didn't turn. She just lifted her hand in a vague gesture, then kept going, unsteady, but still staying on her feet.

Duncan went after her, reaching the door in time to pull it open, watch her step with exaggerated care over the casement step and out into the cold night. There was no one on the side street, and the sky was crystal clear, filled with the brilliance of stars. He walked beside Lauren as she started for the main street, not touching her, but staying close enough that if she started to fall, he could grab her.

They got to the corner without incident and crossed the side street to head south toward the hotel. Lauren managed to walk, only occasionally nearly missing her step before catching herself. Duncan felt tense waiting for her to fall or stumble.

Who would have protected her if he wasn't with her now? Who would have made sure she got home safely, that she didn't stumble and fall? He glanced at her and wondered if she had someone, maybe even a husband waiting back home. He couldn't imagine Lauren not having a man wanting her. "Is there a husband lurking around anywhere?" he asked.

Lauren stopped when Duncan spoke, reached for a wooden porch post for support and held on to it. Her head was swimming and she felt as if she were wrapped in gauze; everything around her was fuzzy and surreal. Drunk. She was drunk. Just what she hadn't wanted to happen, but she could handle the feeling. She just had to walk carefully, and talk slowly to get the words out so he could understand them. "Nope, not even close."

"So, there isn't any involvement, or entanglement, or relationship?"

That about covered her life and for some ridiculous reason, hearing him say it made her eyes smart. "No," she breathed. "Nothing."

"Then it's not just me?"

"What?"

"The no-involvement rule. You didn't make it up for me?"

Yes, she had. Had she said that out loud? No, he was still looking at her, waiting for her to say something. She couldn't get involved with him, period. But that didn't stop the idea from being so seductive. The world was blurry and so was her reasoning, and she wished he'd quit asking questions. "Why don't you just—" She cut off the words before she said them aloud, and swallowed hard.

"Why don't I what?" he asked, and he seemed closer now, inches from her, but she never saw him move.

"Just…just go and find Adrianna," she muttered thickly.

"Why would I do that?"

She shrugged. She didn't know. The thought of him with the tall blonde made her physically sick. Then again, maybe the nausea came from the damn punch. "I don't know. Just…just go and do what you want to do."

"I'm doing what I want to do," he said so softly she wasn't sure she'd heard him right.

"You always do, don't you?" Then she heard herself rattling off things she'd read in his files. "Never marry, never get engaged, do what you want, when you want, and to hell with everyone else. Talk about no involvement."

She saw the dark frown even through the haze of the alcohol and knew she'd said too much. "How in the hell do you know all that about me? I don't remembering giving you a rundown on my past."

Oh, shoot. She'd done it. She'd said things she never should have, and now she had to regroup. But the problem was she couldn't think straight, so she'd go with Vern's advice. "Just stick to the truth."

"It's always a good idea to stick to the truth," Duncan said.

She'd said that out loud! She hadn't meant to. But she had. "Yes…sure," she mumbled. "And I said that…I meant to say, that you…you kissed me, and I knew Adrianna was gone, and I assumed you weren't married." That sounded as clear as mud to her, but shockingly, Duncan seemed to understand what she was saying.

"Okay, you've got a point."

She didn't know what her point was, but she had to stop this conversation from going any further. She turned and started walking again, but slower this time. "I'm drunk," she whispered.

"I think we've agreed on that."

Ignoring him for several minutes while she walked, she had to stop again, for balance, and she reached for the nearest post for support. It was either that or reach for Duncan, and she couldn't do that. She stared down the street at the hotel in the distance. If she could get there, she'd be okay. "I'm never drunk," she mumbled.

"Not your fault," he said. "You didn't know, and Pudge should have warned you about the vodka."

"It's all my fault," she said.

"It's not," Duncan said.

She looked at him, thankful that the shadows hid most of his expression. "You don't know. You don't know at all."

"You've lost me," he said.

"I'm sorry" was the only thing she could think to say. "I…I can't think straight."

"With that much vodka in you, I'm surprised you can think at all."

She could think. She could look at him and think things she shouldn't. Like touching him, being closer, feeling his heat. God, she hoped she hadn't said that out loud. It was time to get to the hotel. "Sure, vodka."

He was so close that she felt him exhale, the warmth of his breath skimming over her cold face. "Come on. Let's get you back to where it's warm."

She didn't move. Instead, she reached out, spreading her hand on his chest. She knew what she was doing. She just couldn't make herself stop. His jacket was thick and there was no way she could feel his heart beating, but that didn't stop her from imagining the beat under her palm. "You're so nice." She meant it. Compared to his father, Duncan was wonderful. No, he was just wonderful on his own. Helping and being there, and not pushing her into anything. "You…you're a good person."

"Oh, don't add that to what you think of me," he murmured.

She patted him once, twice, then drew back, knowing she had to get going in case she said something she wouldn't be able to cover or explain. Drawing back, she walked away from him, toward the hotel.

Come here. Find him. Get him back to L.A. Easy. Get the money. Get out. Simple. But it wasn't. It wasn't simple at all. She tried to walk more quickly, but she couldn't do it. So she just remained as focused as possible on her steps.

"Lauren?" he said. Then, more loudly. "Lauren?"

Duncan took hold of her arms and turned her toward him. "What's going on here?"

"I don't know," she whispered. "It's not right. I'm not right. I think I'm…" She bit her lip. "I don't know. I'm so predictable. So by the rules. No risks. No…risks at all. I mean, by the book. You know." She was babbling and couldn't stop. "Just no risks, no chances. Just play it safe."

Duncan was watching her as if she were mad. And in that moment, the only thing she knew was that she wanted him. She wanted to talk and touch and be with him. And she was terrified that she couldn't make herself move to safety. Not even when he came closer. Not even when the coolness of his hands framed her face. Not even when he bent down and his lips touched hers.

There was heat and urgency in the caress, and she fought against instincts that screamed at her to hold on to him and not let go. She tried to stay very still, not to answer the kiss with a kiss, not to put her arms around him. She tried not to move, and he finally pulled back, his face inches from hers, his breath curling into the frigid air. "This is not playing it safe," he whispered roughly.

She was drunk. That was her excuse. The reason why she let it happen, why she didn't pull back and stop the kiss before it could really begin. Instead, she stood there like some besotted teenager, Duncan against her, and a desire for him a living thing deep inside her soul. If she couldn't think straight before, she couldn't think at all now. "I…no…I can't," she managed to say.

"I know what you told me," he said in a low voice. "But I like taking chances, taking a risk. I always have."

"I can't," she admitted with real honesty.

His hands on her face were all-encompassing and she could barely breathe. "What if I promise to protect you?" he asked roughly. "What if I make sure you won't get hurt?"

She turned from him, breaking all contact, and walked away on unsteady legs. He wouldn't hurt her? That wasn't it at all. He was beside her again, his arm brushing hers, and she hugged her arms around herself as she kept going. She wasn't as drunk now, but she wasn't sober, either. The hotel. She was almost to the door, then Duncan moved past her, opened the door and held it open for her to go inside. The warmth of the lobby almost made her sick to her stomach after the extreme cold outside.

No one was in the lobby and only low night-lights illuminated the area. Lauren hurried to the stairs, going up as quickly as possible, holding on to the railing for dear life. She'd reached her room and almost made it inside when Duncan caught up with her.

"I asked you a question," Duncan said in a low voice.

She wasn't going to play games and ask what the question was because she knew. But it didn't matter what he promised her because she couldn't promise him the same thing. "You won't hurt me," she whispered. "But you don't know me."

"That's the point. I told you, I want to." He came closer, the dim light cutting shadows at his throat and jaw. "I want to, Lauren."

She looked into his dark eyes, then did something she knew she'd regret. She touched his face, lightly, at his jawline, feeling the roughness of a new beard coming in, then her fingers trailed to his lips. She touched the heat there, and trembled. "Don't," she managed to say, but that was all that she said before his lips found hers again.

No! she screamed in her mind, but her body had a will of its own. She sagged into him, her arms lifting to go around his neck, and she parted her lips for him. His body was hard against hers, his taste permeating her being. She responded without the ability not to, pulling him down and closer to her, craving the feeling of him against her, the essence of him in her, and she realized that she was literally jeopardizing everything she'd come here for. And she couldn't. Shouldn't.

Lauren pushed away from him, stumbling, her back hitting the wall. She was barely able to meet his gaze and keep from scrubbing her hand over her mouth. "No, I can't," she whispered, then without looking back closed the door quickly. She tried not to listen for anything outside the room.

She quickly stripped off her clothes, put on the T-shirt she'd discarded earlier, then fell back onto the bed. The room was moving in sickening circles, and she remembered something D.R. had said: "Duncan likes women." She should take advantage of any edge she had to get him back to L.A. The thought clutched at her middle and she rolled onto her side. No, she was not going to let her feelings muddy the waters. She turned on her stomach and buried her face in the pillow. No,

she'd do her job. She'd get to understand him, get him
to go back home, but she wasn't going to hurt anyone,
not anyone. Especially not herself.

Chapter Nine

Lauren fell into a restless sleep, troubled by dreams that made no sense. Duncan, herself, the snow, skiing—and lots of heat. A heat that seemed to filter into her soul and leave her breathless. She woke slowly and reluctantly, aware of sunlight coming in through the dormer window, warmth in the air and her head hurting so badly that it felt ready to explode.

She was hungover. Damn it. She squinted at the clock, relieved to see that she had plenty of time to get up and get to work at Rusty's for the afternoon shift. It was Sunday and they always had a big middle-of-the-day rush, according to Rusty. So she had time to try to get the fuzz out of her head and figure out how she could ever face Duncan again. She got out of bed, careful not to jar her head, grabbed fresh clothes and toiletries and headed downstairs to the bathroom.

She moved slowly down the stairs, and as she reached the second-floor hallway, the door to her old room opened and out stepped the middle-aged man she'd seen in the lobby yesterday. He had an improbable tan, and was wearing very high-end skiing clothes that looked as if they'd never seen a slope in their life. He was short, maybe five-seven or so, and the minute he saw Lauren, he smiled at her.

The smile wasn't pleasant. It was more predatory. Normally she would have been offended. But she looked and felt horrible, and would have laughed if she hadn't known her head would explode if she tried. "Well, well, well," he said, elongating each word, then reaching to close his door without taking his eyes off her. "Good morning, beautiful."

He was blind, too, she thought. "Good morning," she said and quickly went into the bathroom, closing and locking the door behind her.

She heard voices out in the hallway. She couldn't tell what was being said and she didn't care. All she cared about was drinking some water and taking a hot shower. After drinking four full glasses of water, she turned on the shower. Stripping off her robe, she stepped under the warm spray and just stood there.

By the time she stepped out and dried off, she felt a bit more human, but no more ready to face Duncan. Her head still ached, but she could move without too much pain. One look at herself in the mirror over the pedestal sink and she knew that she was never going to drink Pudge's punch again…or any punch unless she knew what was in it. She quickly dried her hair, fluffing it around her face, then got dressed in fresh clothes—jeans and a deep-green cable-knit sweater.

Lauren gathered up her things and hurried back up

to her room. Once she'd put on her jacket and snow boots, she grabbed her running shoes to put on at work.

As she made her way to the lobby, Lauren saw Annie handing out her muffins.

Dressed in jeans and a flannel shirt, Annie was smiling at the guests. "Enjoy the muffins," she said, then turned to Lauren. "Well, it's your lucky day. It's late, but I've got one left, just for you," she said, holding up a plate with a single muffin sitting on it.

"I don't want to take your last muffin," Lauren said.

"Don't worry. I can always make more," she said and handed the muffin to Lauren along with a paper napkin. "Enjoy!"

"Thanks," Lauren said.

"Are you feeling okay?" Annie asked her as she studied her closely. "You look a bit pale."

"I'm fine," she said. "Thanks for the muffin."

"Have a great day."

"Let's hope so," Lauren murmured, then went out into the cold, clear day.

Although the roads and walkways were clear, snow was piled at the curbs and a few cars that hadn't moved were literally snowbound from the plow's swipes. She rolled the muffin in the napkin and pushed it into her jacket pocket, hunched into the slight wind and headed for Rusty's. She could do this. She'd act as if nothing had happened, act like a friend, a co-worker. She'd do it. Or she'd use the drunkenness as an excuse and say she was sorry. Otherwise she'd have to walk away, and she couldn't do that.

When she stepped into Rusty's, her determination

was put to the test. The place was full, but the first person she saw was Duncan. She almost ran into him when she stepped through the door. He stopped inches from her, and she looked up into his dark eyes.

"Good afternoon," he murmured. "How are you feeling?"

"Okay," she said. "But you won't be."

He frowned at her. "Why?"

She reached into her pocket and took out the muffin in the napkin. "*Bon appétit*," she said as she handed it to him. As she headed for the office she thought she heard him laugh.

One of the waitresses had some aspirin, and as time went on, she was grateful she'd taken two of them. She was constantly aware of Duncan—in the kitchen, in the office. By the time she got her next break, he was walking out the door. He never looked back. And here she'd worried about him saying something about the kiss, about the way she'd acted, and he was the one acting as if nothing had happened.

She worked three more hours after her break, and as the customers started to thin out, she took her last break of the day. Sitting in a back booth beyond the fireplace, she sipped a cup of tea and prayed that her head—and her feet—would stop hurting.

As she sat and relaxed a bit, she looked around at the customers in the restaurant. There were maybe fifteen people in all, some couples, some single sitting at the counter, but the rush was over. The diner was calm, but she still felt stressed. That stress had started last night and had only gotten worse. She'd literally circled Duncan's neck with her arms and arched into him. She'd done more than just kiss him.

Unable to drink her tea, she went into the kitchen and put the cup in the wash tray.

Rusty was in there unpacking heads of lettuce. "Rusty?" she said as she went over to him by the counter.

He looked up at her, a head of lettuce in his hand. "Damn good stuff, huh? Green, crisp, really nice. Webb started an early delivery. He has great produce."

"It looks great," she said.

He put the lettuce on the counter. "So, what did you need?"

"Would you mind if I used the phone in your office?" She'd realized she'd left her cell phone at the hotel after already reaching the diner.

"Sure thing," he said before going back to the lettuce.

Closing the door to the office, Lauren called Vern using her calling card. It rang twice before Yolanda, the receptionist, answered. "Sutton Agency, how can I direct your call?"

"Yolanda, it's Lauren. Is Vern in?"

"Just stepped out for dinner with a client. Want me to give him a message or have him contact you when he comes back? I can page him, if it's an emergency."

"Just tell him I'm checking in. Things are going slower than I expected. I'll get back to him tomorrow."

"You got it, Lauren. So, how is it up there? I heard it's real pretty and the skiing is better than Aspen or Tahoe."

"It's nice," she said. "Lots of people, and I'm sure the skiing is great."

"Cool."

She smiled and said, "Freezing, actually. Talk to you later."

She hung up and Duncan entered before she'd even stood up. She stayed where she was as he came in and closed the door behind him. Then he was by the desk, his hair looking slightly mussed, as if he'd carelessly raked his fingers through it. Or—and the next thought made her very uncomfortable—he'd been with someone. Maybe Adrianna? "I'm finished here," she said quickly as she stood, covering a flinch when her headache made itself known. "The office is yours."

"I don't want the office," he said, and the way he said it stopped her in her tracks.

"Excuse me?"

He watched her in silence for a nerve-racking moment, then finally said, "I came in here to talk to you."

Her stomach tightened. "I don't think we need to talk."

"I do." He exhaled and she braced herself, prepared for him to bring up the kiss and her reaction to it. "I told you last night that I wouldn't do anything to hurt you. And you said you were sorry. I was the one who should have said that. I was pushy. I apologize."

She hadn't expected an apology. D. R. Bishop's son was apologizing to her? And he didn't even have a reason. "I was drunk, not you. Now I'm—"

"Not looking for a relationship. I know. And I understand."

"You do?"

"Yes." He smiled slightly, but the expression made

it hard for her to breathe. "I just wanted you to know that I'm sorry."

She stared at him. "Thank you" was all she could think to say.

He came closer, cutting around the corner of the desk to stand within a foot of her, and she wished he hadn't. She didn't want to be this close to him. "Thank goodness that's settled. We got off to a rocky start, so why don't we just forget it?"

She'd been worried all day, wondering how to deal with what she'd done the night before. Now he was letting her off the hook. "Okay," she said, accepting his apology. "We'll forget about it."

"Deal," he said, a slight smile touching his lips now.

She exhaled. "Now, I've got just a little while longer before I can get something to eat and go and soak my sore feet."

"I could use something to eat, too," he said.

She instantly felt tense again, but decided to focus on her job, the one she'd really come to Silver Creek for. "I've got work to do. But if you can wait a bit to eat, I'll be in the back booth in a couple hours."

He lifted one eyebrow, an expression she'd come to recognize. Then he nodded. "Sure. Why not?"

She went around the desk to leave, but Duncan was between her and the door, forcing her to stop if she didn't want to run right into him. That's when she realized he was staring at her lips. Then his gaze lifted to hers. He didn't touch her, but she felt as disoriented as if he had. Without a word, he moved to one side, and she scooted past.

Saying they'd start all over again, that they'd forget about what had happened last night, was foolish. She went down the hallway into the main dining room, knowing that if a look from the man could make her feel as disoriented as a kiss, maybe she'd made another blunder. But before she could cancel dinner, a group of skiers came in and she went back to work.

DUNCAN HUNG OUT in the office for over an hour, reviewing the books that Rusty had left for him, and when he went back out into the restaurant, Lauren was nowhere to be seen. He nodded at a couple who were just leaving, wished them a good day, then headed for the kitchen. The door swung open and Lauren exited with a tray of drinks.

"Oh," she said. "Sorry."

She was about to move past him when he said, "How long until you're off?"

"Fifteen minutes or so."

"Okay," he said and motioned to the back booth where she usually took her breaks. "Meet you over there when you're done. What do you want to eat?"

She hesitated, then said, "Stew in bread. I'll get it—"

"No, I'll get it. You finish up," he said, and went into the kitchen before she could argue with him.

In fifteen minutes, sourdough bread bowls filled with stew sat on the back table as Lauren joined him. She looked tired, and beautiful. She glanced at the food, then reached for her glass, drinking half of the water before setting it down and sitting back in the seat. "Thanks," she said.

He thought he was hungry, but found he didn't have much interest in the food. Duncan wasn't quite sure what had brought on the apology earlier. He felt vaguely out of control, and he didn't like it. "No problem," he said, trying to distract his thoughts. "The stew's good here."

They ate in silence for a bit until Lauren said, "So, does this make us even?"

"Excuse me?" he asked.

"You said you were responsible for me since you saved my life, and I think making this dinner takes you off the hook legally."

He'd forgotten about the foolish rule he'd made up off the top of his head. "I think we can call it even, but I didn't make this. It's Rusty's food, I just served it."

"Serving is as good as making it," she said.

He took a drink of his wine, letting the heat trickle down his throat. Then he sat back, resting the goblet on the table. "Okay, we're even. I'd hate to have that hanging over my head."

She smiled slightly, enough to touch her eyes and lift the corners of her lips. God, she was lovely. Then she held up her water glass toward him in a salute. "I hereby agree that you are off the hook. You are a free man."

He lifted his own glass to touch hers and their fingers brushed as the glasses clinked. The slight contact was like a lightning bolt and he quickly drew back, then drained the rest of his wine. "Good, good," he said, putting the empty glass down next to his stew.

"Good, good," she echoed, then picked up her fork to stir the hot meal.

He looked down at his own food and ate a bit of it before sitting back. "Have you ever skied?"

"Once or twice," she said as she looked up at him with a thick piece of meat speared on her fork. "And I liked it, sort of. But I got so cold, and so wet, I was miserable before I got the hang of it." She nibbled on the meat and looked relieved. "This is actually pretty good."

"You sound surprised."

"I wasn't sure if I could…" She bit her lip.

"Pretty bad hangover, huh?"

She blushed slightly. "You could say that."

"The cotton mouth, the headache, the stomach that won't settle?"

"You sound as if you know all about it," she said before eating the last of her meat morsel.

"Been there, done that," he said.

"No wonder we sell so much of this stew." She leaned across the table. "Have you tasted Rusty's vegetable soup? It's fantastic."

Duncan looked around the room. With the rush over, the diner was pretty quiet. "It's a good place."

"It is." She played with her stew, pushing it around now before she speared a carrot with her fork. "Since we're starting over, can I ask you something?"

He wasn't sure he wanted to have her delving into what made him tick, but he shrugged. "Okay."

"Why are you here at Rusty's?"

He could answer that. "It's the first place I walked into when I got to town, and I stayed." He mimicked her actions, stirring his stew, but he didn't get anything with his fork. "I liked it. Rusty needed help and I decided to stay around for a while."

"What do you do here?"

"A bit of everything. Whatever Rusty needs."

"What does Rusty need?"

"Help from time to time."

She frowned. "You know, you'd make a great politician."

"What?"

"You can say a lot, without really saying anything."

He had no doubt he was double-talking. He had no desire to outline why he was here and what he was doing. "There isn't much to say. I'm just here for now."

"Then what?"

"I'll move on, probably. I'm not sure." He'd thought of leaving from time to time, but always found a reason to stick around. Right now, Lauren was part of that reason. "How about you? How long are you staying?"

She looked down at her stew, then set down her fork, ripped a piece of the bread off the bowl and popped in into her mouth. After she chewed and drank some water, she finally spoke. "I don't know."

"No plans?"

"No, not yet." She eyed him again, ignoring her food now. "You look as though you always have plans, as though you know where you're going."

She couldn't be more wrong. "No more than most people."

"How old are you?" she asked suddenly.

"How old are you?"

"Old enough."

"Me, too."

She smiled. "And here I thought women were the ones who were vain."

"It has nothing to do with vanity. I just didn't know what your question had to do with what we're talking about."

"Okay, I was thinking, at your age, which I'd guess was mid-thirties, most people have settled in for their lives."

He had thought he had, too, then found out how wrong that assumption had been. "I guess I'm going through a stage."

"Self-discovery?"

He almost laughed, but stopped when he realized that maybe that was a good tag to put on what he was doing. "Maybe."

"What about your past? Was it good or bad?"

He wasn't comfortable with where this was going, but he tried to answer her. "It was good. It was bad. Like anyone's life."

"Why did you leave it?"

She was hitting all the buttons, yet she looked so innocent, just talking over dinner. "I wanted to," he said and deliberately got up and headed to the kitchen to refill his wineglass. By the time he returned, he'd hoped the discussion was closed, but he had no such luck.

"So, why did you want to leave?" she asked, picking up where she'd left off.

He narrowed his eyes at her. She'd torn off the top

rim of her bread bowl and hardly touched the stew. He motioned to it. "I thought you liked the stew."

"I do," she said. "But I'm full."

"You've been eating the bowl."

She blinked, then suddenly laughed, a soft, lovely sound. "I guess I am." She dropped the piece of bread she had in her fingers, then brushed her hands together. "So, why did you take off and come here?"

He'd had enough. He didn't want to go through this with her, and he wasn't going to. "Forget it. It's not important."

"So much for getting to know you," she said and stood.

Just like that, the humor was gone, and he didn't like it. He got up to face her. "I didn't say we had to bare our souls, did I?" There was more of an edge to his voice than he'd intended.

Color flooded her cheeks and her lashes lowered to partially hide her lavender eyes. "I'm tired, and I've got an early day again tomorrow."

"Sure," he said. He turned and motioned to the other waitress. "We're done," he said and dropped a couple bills on the table. "I'll get our jackets," he said, turning from her and heading to the office.

On his way back to Lauren, he ran into Rusty.

"I thought you'd left earlier," Rusty said.

"I did, then came back to check the ledger you left for me. I wanted to let you know I won't be around tomorrow."

"So, you're going to disappear again?"

Duncan shrugged. "Just take some time to think."

"You do a lot of that. Got any answers yet?"

Not even close. "No, not yet, but I'm trying."

Rusty patted his shoulder. "That's all any of us can do," he said and went into his office.

Duncan turned and met Lauren by the front door. Handing over her jacket, they made their way out to the evening streets. They walked side by side toward the hotel, not talking until Lauren finally spoke up. "I'm sorry if I was being too pushy, or said the wrong thing."

He stopped and so did she, facing each other the way they had the night before. "Just what do you think you said that was wrong?"

She shrugged. "I don't know. You tell me."

"Nothing," he said and turned to walk again.

She fell in step with him, their sleeves brushing from time to time, and despite the fleeting nature of the contact, every time it happened, it jolted his nerves. She didn't speak, didn't press him for more explanations, and for some reason that made him want to tell her about walking out on his father, and ending up here. But he kept quiet until they were inside the hotel and on the second floor outside his room.

She turned to him in the soft light, flipping the hood off her rich hair, and he knew she was the first and probably only person he wanted to tell about his life back in L.A. He hadn't felt this connection with anyone, until Lauren. And now he knew if he wanted anything with her, he'd have to explain who he really was.

Chapter Ten

For all his resolution to tell Lauren the truth, Duncan
didn't get the chance. A voice echoed in the hallway and
he and Lauren turned to see Linus Kendall, a CPA who
had the room next to his, at the top of the stairs. The man
was holding on to the top post, and Duncan could tell
the guy was drunk—just the way he'd been the first time
they'd met. He could smell the alcohol even from where
he stood, and he could see a stain on the front of the
bright-blue ski outfit—probably from the alcohol.

Linus swayed before steadying himself with a grip
on the newel post. "Well, well, well," he muttered
thickly. "So, you got…" He cleared his throat and
brushed his free hand across his face, then wagged his
forefinger in Duncan's direction. "You sly devil, you,"
he mumbled. "And here…I thought…you were with
that other…the lush…luscious one."

Duncan frowned, with little or no patience for the
man. "What are you talking about?"

"At the lodge…you and her…" He licked his lips.
"What a knockout." He grinned at Lauren. "Not that

you're not," he said to her, then turned back to Duncan. "Two of 'em…" His voice was getting thicker, and Duncan wished he'd just shut up. "Blond, red…" He hiccuped sharply. "Wow, dude. You're awesome."

Adrianna. This man had seen him at the lodge with Adrianna. He felt Lauren intently watching the two of them. "You're mistaking me for someone else."

Linus shrugged. "I thought…it was you, but…" He shrugged again. "Don't know…"

"Do you need some help getting to your room?" Duncan asked, wishing he'd just disappear.

Very slowly, Linus let go of the banister, then just as slowly walked with exaggerated care toward the door to his room. "I can manage," he muttered as he reached for the door latch. He exhaled and the smell of stale alcohol drifted in their direction as he fumbled to get a key out of his pocket, then struggled to get it into the lock.

Duncan finally went over, took the key and unlocked the door. "There you go. It's open."

Linus grabbed the key and Duncan moved aside to let him into his room. The man shifted, muttered, "Thanks," grabbed the door latch and looked at the two of them. "You sly fosh…fo-fox," he mumbled thickly. "You two go and—" He never finished because he tumbled out of sight into his room. There was a thud, then his disembodied voice called out, "I'm okay. Jush fine…fine." Then the door slammed shut.

Duncan looked back at Lauren and her lavender eyes were wide as they stared at the closed door. "Do you think he's okay?"

"I don't think he's feeling anything right now." There was a muffled crashing sound from behind the closed door. "And I'm sure he didn't feel that, either."

Lauren giggled. "I hope not." She looked up at him. "I thought you said Adrianna was gone."

"I told you she wanted me to help with the skier. She was staying at the inn, but hopefully she's on her way to Switzerland with Fritz or Erik or Claus or whatever his name is. The guy must have seen me there with her." He shook his head. "She's not important, Lauren, trust me."

"I didn't mean to pry. As you said, we aren't baring our souls."

No, they weren't, and his earlier idea of telling her the truth had passed. "No, of course not."

"What were you saying before he interrupted?"

"It's not important," he said, lying.

She studied him for a long moment, then touched his arm lightly. Even through the thick jacket, the contact made him tense. "Are you sure?"

He lied again. "I'm sure."

She drew back and didn't argue. "Okay, then I guess I'll go to my room. I'll see you tomorrow?"

"I'll be gone tomorrow," he said. She stopped and looked back at him.

"You taking off again?"

"I've got things to do."

She nodded and turned, heading up and out of sight. He waited in the hallway until he heard her door open and close, then he went into his own room. Linus was silent next door. Duncan didn't bother turning on any lights. He had no idea that anyone he knew had seen him with Adrianna, but it didn't matter. She wasn't important. The bottom line was, he didn't care. He wished her well, but that was it. And Linus was no one to him. Just a drunk in Silver Creek trying to get over a divorce.

It was Lauren he was worried about, whom he thought about. He stripped off his clothes and went into the bathroom to take a shower. He went over and over his conversation with Lauren at the diner and wondered what would have happened if he'd told her everything.

Once out of the shower, Duncan toyed with the idea of going to the Briar, but decided not to. He got into bed, stretched out and stared at the ceiling. He'd almost told her everything. Odd, but it had seemed very right to do that. He'd think about it more, and maybe tomorrow when he went to the cabin, the one place he could be totally alone and get his thoughts in order, he'd have some answers.

LAUREN WOKE AT DAWN, her sleep fragmented and something less than restful. Duncan had been ready to talk to her last night. He'd been so close to opening up before the drunk had appeared and ruined everything. She lay in bed, thinking. He wasn't going to be around today. Again. If it wouldn't jeopardize her cover, she'd follow him. Where was he going? If Adrianna was gone, and Lauren had no reason to think he was lying to her, then who was he going to see, or what was he going to do?

She got out of bed and headed for the bathroom. She didn't have to be at work until two for the late lunch and dinner shift, so she had time to take care of some basic things. Like make a call to Vern. Maybe get more information on Duncan.

A half hour later, she'd showered and dressed in jeans, a heavy sweater and boots. She pushed her cell phone into her pocket, grabbed her heavy jacket and left. Once she'd made her way to the lobby, she found it empty. Stepping out into the bitter cold, Lauren made her way to the parking area where she'd left her car that first night. Duncan's car was parked there, too. His was clear of snow, and she saw someone brushing at hers with a large broom.

She hadn't met Annie's husband, but she'd bet that was him—a tall man dressed in a plaid wool jacket, big boots and a red ski cap. She walked over to where he was pushing at the snow on her rear window. "Hello there."

He turned and she noticed he had hawkish features and a thick, dark mustache. "Good morning. Bet you're Lauren."

"Yes, I am."

"I'm Rick, Annie's husband. I meant to get this cleared yesterday, but never made it out here. It's about done, though."

"I appreciate it," she said.

He turned and pushed at the last of the snow blocking the back window, then pulled the broom back. The front window, both side windows and the rear window were clear, but the rest of the car was still thick with snow. "Flip on the defrost as soon as you can, and you'll be fine."

"Thanks so much," she said and took the key out of her pocket. She pushed it in the lock, and had to struggle a bit before she heard a click. She grabbed the handle and tugged the door open, climbing in to sit on the cold leather seats. "Thanks again," she said to Rick.

"Oh, hey, if you want to wait a minute, I'll run in and get you some of Annie's muffins to take with you."

"Oh, no, I'm in a hurry," she said. "But thanks for offering."

She smiled, then swung her door shut and watched Rick go into the hotel. When she tried to start the engine, though, nothing happened. Was this a cosmic joke being played on her as punishment for pretending to have trouble that first day? "Come on, you can of bolts," she muttered and turned the key again. This time it cranked weakly, then kicked over and roared to life.

"Sorry for that comment," she muttered as she adjusted the heater and waited until the air from the vents started to feel vaguely warm. Putting the car in gear, Lauren backed out of the parking lot and headed toward the street.

Her call to Vern wouldn't take up too much time, and once she spoke with him she'd go up to the inn and see if she could get in and look around. She was curious about what it was like and how the "beautiful" people vacationed. She drove slowly with the flow of the traffic, then spotted a drive-through restaurant that was open and advertised the Best Coffee in Silver Creek.

Once she had the coffee, Lauren circled back to the street. Sipping the hot coffee as she drove, she'd just reached the inn's entrance when the car faltered, then caught. A few moments later it started to lose power and she ended up gliding to the side of the road.

The car stopped on its own and sat idling before it coughed, missed, then stalled. She started it—it died. She started it. It died. Then it wouldn't start at all and she sank back into the seat with a frustrated sigh. "You useless, annoying beast," she muttered at the car. The car was dead and this time Duncan Bishop wasn't coming to her rescue.

Her breath curled in the icy air as she tried to figure out her next move. Popping the hood, she got out into the cold and hurried to the front of the car. No loose wires or bad connections as far as she could tell.

She got back in the car, leaving the hood up, then reached for her cell phone. Once she'd gotten the number from Information, she dialed Rollie's Garage.

"Rollie's Garage. Rollie speaking."

"Hi, Rollie, this is Lauren Carter." She knew the best way to identify herself to Rollie. "I work at Rusty's Diner and I've got the classic—"

"Hey, I remember you. How's that car of yours?"

"It's dead."

She could have sworn she heard a slight gasp of horror over the line. "You didn't have an accident, did you?"

"Oh, no. I was driving, and it lost power, then died. I'm stuck on the side of the road."

"Where are you?"

"A quarter of a mile or so from the main entrance to The Inn at Silver Creek."

"You wait right there. I'm coming," he said and hung up.

She hung up, too, then sat back in the car, hugging her arms around herself and waiting. A couple luxury cars went past and turned in farther up at the inn. Her mother had told her once never to pretend something bad was happening because sooner or later it would happen for real. Well, her mother had been right.

She reached for her coffee, thankful it was still fairly hot, the windows in the car fogging up as she waited. Her feet grew colder by the minute. But after five minutes or so, she heard a heavy engine approaching. Swiping to clear her window, Lauren saw a tow truck slowly driving past her. It pulled in ahead, then backed up toward her car. She put her empty coffee cup back on the seat and got out of the car. Even with the sun shining brightly, it was freezing outside. She made her way toward the tow truck.

But she stopped when she heard another car coming. Turning as it pulled in behind her car, Lauren saw it was Duncan's SUV with its torn-up side. He stopped and got out of his car, the watch cap pulled low. "I didn't think there could be two cars like this anywhere in the area."

"What are you doing here?" she asked.

"I was at Rollie's when the call came in." He glanced at her car. "Temperamental again?"

"Downright rotten at the moment," she said.

He stopped in front of her and smiled. "Rotten, huh?"

"Very."

"I'll take a look at her," Rollie called to them and ducked his head under the hood.

"Why do men always call cars by the feminine pronoun?"

Duncan chuckled roughly. "Because they're temperamental with a mind of their own?"

"Don't go down that road," she murmured, but couldn't help smiling a bit herself.

He studied her from under lowered lashes. "Feeling better today?"

"I'm fine," she said.

"Well, we've got a problem," Rollie said as he made his way over to them. "Looks like she's got a bad fuel pump, and even worse, she's picky. That pump has to be ordered in. I can't get it until tomorrow or the next day."

"Any idea how much it's going to cost?"

"None. Could be pricey," he said.

"Well, I need it, so go ahead and order it," Lauren said. "Just fix it as soon as you can."

"No problem. All I need is the key to tow it back for you."

"It's in the ignition," she said. "Can I get a ride back with you?"

"Sure, as soon as I get it hitched onto the truck."

"I'll give you a ride to wherever you were going," Duncan said, startling her with his offer.

"I wasn't going anywhere in particular, just getting some fresh air."

"I can drive you to fresh air." Before she could reject his offer, his voice lowered. "Lauren, we started talking last night, and I'd like to finish that talk." She hoped she didn't look as stunned as she felt. She'd been trying to figure out how to get him to talk again, and hadn't come up with any ideas. Now he was handing her the chance. "It won't take long," he said.

"I…sure, okay." She turned and called to Rollie, "I'll ride with Duncan."

He waved to her. "I'll let you know when she's ready."

"Thanks so much," she said.

"Ready?" Duncan asked her.

She wasn't sure, but she wasn't going to let this opportunity slip past, either. "Ready," she said and followed him to his SUV. He opened the passenger door for her to climb into the car, then went around to get behind the wheel. The warmth in the car felt wonderful, and more heat came flowing out of the vents when Duncan started the engine.

"Do you need more heat?"

"No, it's perfect," she said as they drove by the tow truck and waved to Rollie. "I was freezing in my car."

They were heading north, away from Silver Creek. "Where were you going?"

"Just up the way," she said vaguely.

She clasped her hands in her lap and stared ahead of them on the snowy road. How long had she known him? Not long at all. They'd kissed. They'd talked. Then they'd been interrupted. Now he wanted to finish their earlier talk. And she had hopes that he'd tell her about him leaving L.A. But he drove quietly and made no effort to start talking.

Lauren had to force herself not to push, not to ask what he wanted to say. She was going to let him begin, let him lay down the ground rules. She wasn't going to blow this chance.

"So, the car's dead?" he asked, startling her slightly with the sound of his voice in the quietness around them.

"Really dead. I just hope it won't be too expensive to fix."

He drove slowly along the road. "Knowing Rollie, he'll probably pay you for the honor of fixing her."

"What is it with calling the car 'her' and drooling over the darn thing?"

"Your brother, the one who fixed it up, what did he call her…or it?"

She could talk about this, tell the truth, and hopefully let him feel comfortable telling her things about himself. "Honestly, he called the car Suzie Q, and don't ask me why or where it came from. Alan always has a name for his cars, and they're always female. Go figure."

"How about your other brothers? Are they into cars?"

"No, Alan's the only one. Cars are his life. He's two years older than me, and I'd say he has had maybe twenty cars, most of which he's restored or repaired or both. Joe's two years older than Alan, and he's a high-school science teacher near San Francisco, and Tim's the oldest boy."

"What does Tim do?"

"He's a doctor."

"Specialist?"

"Nope, an old-fashioned general practitioner who works at a clinic in Oregon."

"What about your parents?"

"They live in Oregon, and my father's retired. They're enjoying life, from what they tell me."

"So, you had an Ozzie and Harriet kind of family?"

"Gosh, no. My family's had trouble." She measured her words carefully. "My brothers fight with each other, and with me, and they've been in their share of scrapes, but we always managed to make up. Family's important." She hoped he'd reveal his own thoughts about his family. One thing she'd known instinctively when she hired on with Vern was that there were a lot of nonverbal responses to what another person said. "You know how families can be? Fighting and feuding, but that doesn't stop you from being a family."

"Is that the way it works?" he asked.

"That's the way it works for us, but then again, I never said we were normal."

He chuckled roughly. "Normal? Now there's a word that can mean just about anything, can't it?"

"Exactly." She looked outside at the stone fence surrounding the inn. "That place behind the fence is far from normal."

He gave a passing glance at the fence, then looked back at the road. "I think that's why people go there, because they can afford to do away with normal and get pampered, instead. That's why Adrianna was staying there. Money, privacy, luxury."

"Adrianna must be loaded." From what she'd read about the Barr family, *loaded* was putting it mildly.

"She's got more money than most people will see in a lifetime."

"So, you were after her money?" Lauren hoped teasing him would lighten the mood.

It worked. He laughed. "God, no. She's fun, and smart, and we had a good time. While it lasted." His laughter was fading. "I told you, she's moved on."

"Until she has a falling-out with her ski bum?"

"He's a Swiss skiing champion."

This was her moment to take a chance. "Tell me something?"

He cast her a slanting glance, then looked back at the road and nodded. "If I can."

She had to force her hands to relax when she realized she was clenching them in her lap. "Why did Adrianna follow you to Silver Creek and hunt you down if she's so over you?"

"She didn't know I was here. She came with Erik or Fritz or Hans, to have some fun, and we ran into each other by accident."

"You were never here with her?" she asked, even though she knew he hadn't been in Silver Creek since birth.

"No, it was just chance. She was here. I was here. We were at the same store at the same time. End of story."

"She came for fun. Why did you come?"

"I was born here," he said without missing a beat.

She was surprised that he told her that bit of information so easily. "You were coming home?"

He flexed his hands on the steering wheel and he slowed his speed as they started to climb. "No. This isn't home. I left here when I was one week old. No, it's not home," he repeated. He slowed more, then swung left onto a narrow road that had recently been plowed, leaving just enough room for two cars to pass on the pavement. He stopped talking and watched the road, shifting gears for the climb.

"You said you wanted to finish what you were saying last night?"

The only noise when her words faded off was the sound of the SUV, its motor and the crunch of the tires on the pavement. She waited, watching Duncan, the narrowing of his eyes, the way his jaw was set. When she couldn't take it any longer, she finally asked, "Did I misunderstand what you said back there?"

"No. I was just trying to figure out how to explain things to you." He shrugged. "Basically, I'm here because I walked out on my old life. I let go of that life because I didn't want to be a part of it any longer." She didn't miss the way he flexed his hands on the steering wheel before re-gripping it. "I left."

This was what she'd been waiting for, and no drunk was going to interrupt them this time. "Just like that? One day you woke up and said to yourself, it's time to leave?"

"It wasn't that simple, or that neat. It happened over a period of time."

"Who did you leave behind?" she asked softly.

He stared at the road ahead of them as it wound gradually upward. "My father. And everything he stands for."

"I can't imagine doing that," she said truthfully. "I mean, an argument is one thing, but to just leave? It must have been really important for you to do that."

"You have to know my father to understand. Things are different with him. Physically, he's a big man, with an even bigger ego, never finished high school, but knows more than anyone about anything. Or so he thinks. He oversees one of the biggest corporations in the world, and he does it by running roughshod over anyone and everyone. Subtlety isn't his forte. There's always a right way—his way. He assumed I saw things his way, that I'd stick with him no matter what, and when he stepped down, I'd take up his banner and trample the masses."

His words could have applied to the Duncan Bishop she'd read about, but not the Duncan Bishop sitting next to her. She'd come here assuming he'd been shaped in the image of his father. Tough, deadly, a killer instinct. But that wasn't who she'd met in Silver Creek. "You're his son."

He exhaled harshly. "I am. I'm like him in more ways than I'd like to be. But I couldn't continue to support what he was doing."

She watched him carefully, and kept the next question simple and direct. "What did he do?"

Chapter Eleven

Duncan had never been the type to confide in anyone, to talk out personal problems or ideas. He just did things, fixed things and then got on with his life. But he could literally feel the tension he'd carried for six months starting to seep away simply by confessing what had happened in L.A. Saying the words changed everything, especially saying them to Lauren.

He released a low rushing hiss of air, and more tension left with it. He wanted to tell her the truth. "To make this simple, my father and I had a discussion about some business practices. I told him he'd gone too far. He disagreed and wouldn't change his mind. It's his business, so I left."

He knew she was watching him, taking in everything he said. "But you walked out on your father, not just his business, didn't you?"

"I did. Our issues went beyond business, although he'd swear that's all it was. He crossed a line, and I couldn't cross it with him. There is…or was, a company that he'd had his eye on for a while. Not the whole company, exactly, but a division that he thought we needed. He bid on it, was rejected and wouldn't take no for an answer."

"That sounds like business to me."

"It's more than that. The man who ran the other company was a friend. We'd known him for years. He'd put his life into his business, and he wanted to keep it whole, not break it up, thereby weakening it. My father didn't think twice about setting out to destroy the whole company just to get that single division. He was ready to destroy everything that got in his way."

"And you never did that?"

He grimaced, but told the truth. "Sure I did. I went right along with his plans, saw the light at the end of the tunnel and justified crushing everything between us and that light, every time. Damn, I was good at it. But when it came to that last deal, I just couldn't go through with it. He'd gone too far. I tried to reason with him, to get him to back off, but he refused. The bottom line is, and was, it's his company. It's his empire, his dominion, and he's the king. With one swipe of his hand, he'd lop off heads and never blink."

"You told him how you felt?"

"Over and over again." He slowed down, easing the SUV around a sharp curve in the narrow road, and sounded his horn in case another car was heading toward them. "His only concern was me being too damn soft." Duncan was holding on to the steering wheel so tightly his hands ached. "You know, I'm not noble, or better than him. I just suddenly realized that there was a line I wouldn't cross, and he already had."

"You walked away from everything and came to Silver Creek?"

"I never even thought about coming here at first. I traveled, took care of loose ends, did a lot of thinking. Eventually I decided to come here for a while."

The scenery was more rugged now, and the first time he'd seen it, he'd been awestruck by its beauty. At that moment, he barely noticed it. "I've stuck around longer than I intended to," he admitted.

"Why?"

He shrugged. "I've got things to do."

She didn't ask him what things, but instead asked, "Any regrets?"

Regrets. The word was burned into his mind. Hell, he had more than most, he imagined. But he knew leaving L.A. wasn't one of them. "Why would I?" he asked, with just a touch of defensiveness.

"You left your father. You said you don't have siblings, and it sounds as if he's about all you have, and you're about all he has. It must be hard, and it must make you wonder about things."

Laid out like that, he sounded like a heartless bastard, a holier-than-thou jerk. He'd done everything his father had, in spades, and he was telling Lauren he'd had a moral crisis. He stopped the car in the middle of the road, letting it idle, and turned to her. His eyes met hers, and he could almost see his soul reflected in them. He didn't like it. "What do you think I should be doing, eating my heart out over what I did? Over what my father wouldn't do?" The words were harsher than he'd intended, but she didn't flinch. "You think I'm a heartless bastard, don't you?"

Color touched her cheeks and he knew he'd gone too far. All she'd wanted to know was why he was here. She didn't give a damn about his soul. "No, I don't," she said.

"Listen to me, Lauren. For thirty-eight years I did what I thought I should do, what I had to do. And in that moment, the last time I saw my father, I knew it had all been a mistake. Sure, I regret a hell of a lot of things that I've done in my life, and maybe, on some level, I regret that I left. But trust me, my father didn't give a damn about anything except that next deal." He shook his head sharply. "I'm out of that world, and I'm here for now." He turned away from her and started driving again.

"Where do you go from here?"

"I don't know."

The release he felt by telling her was fading, and he was starting to feel tight inside again. Why should it matter what she thought, right? It shouldn't. But it did, and that made his head ache. He glanced at her. She was staring at her hands in her lap. It mattered. It was that simple.

"I'm sorry," she breathed.

He didn't want an apology. He hadn't done this for sympathy. Why he'd confessed all this, he wasn't sure. Then her eyes met his and the truth was there. He'd wanted her from the first, pure and simple, but now he knew that he wanted more than that.

"Don't feel sorry for me," he said. "My father sure as hell isn't sorry for anything he's ever done. Despite the old poem's assertion, he *is* an island unto himself.

My leaving didn't affect him. There isn't anything else to say."

He spotted the driveway to his cabin and turned into it. Huge pines laden with snow canopied above the path. They crested at the top of the drive where the plow had obviously stopped, depositing a three-foot dump of snow. Beyond was the cabin, a small place built of stone and logs.

"We're here," he said as he turned off the SUV. "All the fresh air anyone could want." He rested his hands on the top of the steering wheel, then looked at her again.

"Where is here?" she asked.

"Miles past the inn. You can actually walk to the top of the road, walk through the trees and see the inn down below."

"It's nice," Lauren murmured, glancing at the cabin. She saw a wraparound porch, windows that were frosted over and a stone chimney in the center of the roof. It was nice, but she hardly gave it a thought.

She was having a hard time absorbing what Duncan had just told her, and making small talk was becoming more difficult. Duncan Bishop was not the arrogant jerk she'd expected to find. Instead, he was a man who had found his own conscience. A man who had walked away when he couldn't accept what he was asked to do. Knowing what she knew now, Lauren needed to take a different tack.

They climbed out of the SUV. Lauren tried not to step into the deep snowbank and stayed as close to the big car as possible. When she reached the front of the

SUV, she came face to face with Duncan. He stood there, a foot away, and her heart literally lurched in her chest. There was no going back, but there was no future with Duncan, either. She wasn't sure what she felt for him, but lying to him about who she was wouldn't help their situation.

She looked away quickly. "Whose place is this?"

"Mine."

Since she hadn't read anything about him owning a cabin, he must have rented it. But this tiny place surely wasn't typical of what a Bishop would rent. And if he owned it, why? He'd said he was going to leave, that he hadn't intended to stay here very long. And if he had a cabin, why was he staying at the hotel?

"Lots of fresh air," he murmured.

She turned and saw his face lifted to the clear light that sneaked in between the branches of the pines, and she felt confused. Narrowed eyes, a strong jaw, a pulse beating at the base of his throat where his jacket parted. A man who made an impression and would never be ignored. But not in the way his father demanded attention. Not even close.

"How do we get to the cabin?" she asked, turning to the piled snow.

"Follow me," he said. They walked to the edge of the bank where a narrow path had been cleared to the cabin's stairs. "Just stay in the cleared path," he called to her over his shoulder as he kept going.

Once they reached the door and made their way inside, Lauren got her first glimpse of how rustic this place really was. A single room was built around a see-through fireplace made of rough river stone. It divided the room in half, with a couch and chairs facing the hearth. She could see a bed in the back, made up with a multicolored quilt, lots of pillows and an iron bed frame painted deep green.

To the right was a kitchen area, with a few cupboards, a stove and refrigerator. The window above the single sink was all but covered by a snowdrift. There was nothing to her left, except some stacked wood under another window that was totally blocked by snow.

Lauren swung the door shut behind her as she went farther into the dark room. "You rent this?"

"No, I bought it," he said.

"Why?" she asked.

He took his time stepping out of his heavy boots and nudging them toward the wall by the door, then crossed to the hearth and spoke over his shoulder. "I wanted to," he said simply. "I saw it one day when I was driving and it was for sale. I liked it. So I bought it."

"But you said you were going to leave Silver Creek sooner or later."

"I will, but for now, I have this."

"Then why don't you live here instead of the hotel?"

He shrugged. "I need to be closer to Rusty's and with our weather, you can get stranded up here."

"Why are we here now?" she asked.

He crouched by the hearth and grabbed a couple logs to make a fire. "I was here earlier and was on my way back from the store when I saw you."

Glancing at the kitchen, she noted a couple plates and cups drying on the counter. Then she looked past the fireplace at the bed. It was made, but the quilt was crooked and one of the pillows had a slight impression in it. This was where he took off to, where he disappeared to when he needed time alone. "It's freezing in here," she said.

He glanced over his shoulder and said, "Turn on the light by the refrigerator, and I'll get the fire going."

She could see her breath curl in the cold air each time she exhaled as she crossed and flipped a wall switch by the refrigerator. An old fixture over the sink flashed on, giving off a bit of light. Moving to stand behind Duncan, Lauren watched him build a fire, taking in the way his jacket strained across his shoulders as he reached for a match from a tin on the hearth. He struck it on the stone, then touched it to the kindling. It flamed, sizzled, then caught and leaped up around the logs.

She moved to crouch by him on his left and held her hands out to the new fire. He shifted and she was aware of the way he pressed his hands to his thighs—strong hands with no rings, blunt nails and tanned skin. Hands that looked like he worked for a living, and not the hands his father had. She remembered clearly shaking D.R.'s hand and thinking in passing that his skin was too smooth. How odd that she remembered that now.

She looked at the fire. "Boy, that's a great fire," she said as the flames licked up and around the dried logs. "It must have been a snap to get your fire badge in Boy Scouts."

"I'm no Boy Scout," he said as he stood and she followed suit, looking up at him. He was watching the fire build, the reflection of the flames flickering in his dark eyes. "I was never a Boy Scout."

She had to get him talking again if she was ever going to convince him to return to L.A. "I know you said you didn't want to talk about this anymore, and it's probably none of my business, but it seems to me that the sensible thing to do would be to just go back, talk to your father, get things settled, then do what you want to do with your life."

"There's nothing sensible when it comes to D. R. Bishop. Getting things settled with him is not possible, unless you agree with him, and do what he demands."

He'd finally said his father's name. She didn't have to feign surprise. "Your father is D. R. Bishop? You walked away from the Bishop empire?"

"Don't sound so impressed." He turned from her and crossed to the kitchen area, pulling open the cupboard doors one after the other. "I took the easy way out. I just walked away."

"I don't know about that. It must have been awfully hard to turn your back on everything you had there," she said and moved closer to where he stood.

"Why? It was all his to begin with. I left it all with him," he said as he closed the cupboard that held canned goods. She stood by the refrigerator. "If I'd been a better person, I would have stayed and fought a bloody, losing battle to stop the deal."

She pushed further. "If you could change it all, would you go back?"

"That's not an option," he said dismissively. "Now,

can we change the subject? I really am through dis-
cussing my father."

"Just one more thing?" she asked, not about to let go
just yet.

"Okay, depending on what it is." He faced her, leaning back against the counter and crossing his arms on
his chest. "Shoot."

"Does your dad know where you are?"

"He can find out anytime he wants to, and he will
eventually, when it suits his purposes, or maybe because he hates to have anything happen that isn't under
his control."

"What happens when he finds you?"

"That's more than one more question," he murmured.

She shrugged. "Sorry."

"It doesn't matter. I'll deal with him, if or when I
have to."

"Isn't going back the easiest way to handle this?"

"Easier said than done," he said, then held up one
hand toward her, palm out. "Now, enough of this."

She didn't argue. "Okay, what subject do you want
to discuss?"

"Fresh air." He stood straight. "I thought that's what
you were looking for."

"Absolutely," she said, then noticed the skiing equip-
ment on a rack by the door. "But if you're thinking of
skiing, count me out." She needed to think, to figure out
what she'd just been told and make it fit with what she
knew. She also needed to get some space from Duncan.
Being in the small cabin was starting to feel uncomfort-

able. "But if you want to, go ahead and I'll just walk around outside and explore the area."

But he didn't give her a chance to do any figuring. "Come on and I'll give you a bird's-eye view of the inn."

"You don't have to," she said.

"I want to." He headed for the door and opened it. Lauren hadn't realized how warm it had grown in the cabin until she stepped back outside. The cold air hurt her face as she made her way down the stairs. Sun bounced off the snow. The trees were bent under the weight of the whiteness that clung to their boughs.

Duncan brushed her arm as he went past her down the steps. He tugged his watch cap lower and exhaled, his breath curling into the frigid air as he looked back up at her. The light exposed lines that were etched around his mouth, and shadowed his jawline. She'd heard more than she'd thought he'd ever tell her, maybe even more than she needed to know. His confession tugged at her, filling her with an unexpected degree of sadness.

Was it just stubbornness, or pigheadedness, on both sides? Was the old man right, that his son should be in the business? Or had the son been right to walk away? Was his battle with morality real or just a ploy?

"I smell fresh air," she said, trying to get her mind around both sides of the situation.

She went down the steps toward him and together they made their way to the promised view. Being close to him wasn't a good idea. Being in the cabin with him had been a particularly bad idea. A job that had seemed so cut-and-dried at the beginning had changed into something much more complicated.

She looked everywhere but at him—at the towering trees overhead and at the sky beyond starting to darken with gathering clouds.

"This is so incredible," she said.

He didn't respond and she didn't look at him. She kept going, exerting herself in an effort to ignore the way he made her feel. She understood why he'd walked out. She understood why he felt he had no reason to go back. And maybe she would have done the same thing in the same situation.

They continued to climb up the hill. Duncan stayed right beside her, and was silent. To their left was a steep bank, and to the right was a drop-off to a shallow ravine. They kept walking until they reached the spot where the clearing ended. A huge mound of snow blocked the route. Beyond, the road was hidden under the fallen snow.

Duncan went past her, climbing, kicking at the snow, exposing rocks underneath. He climbed over the rocks, then turned and held his hand out to her. "Come on. The view is unbelievable. It's worth the effort."

She looked up at him. "The view from where?"

"The top of the world," he said, motioning behind him with his head. "It's easy."

All she could see was a rocky bank and heavy, heavy trees. "Easy for you to say," she muttered, then reached up and took his hand.

His fingers closed over hers strongly, surely, and for a flashing moment, she had the most incredible sense of being safe. He pulled her up, and after she scrambled to reach him he steadied her by placing his other hand around her waist. When she looked up, she felt anything but safe. She was terrified, because this was the only place she wanted to be, the only place in the world she felt she belonged.

Before she could do anything stupid, Lauren pulled free of his hold on her, gulping for air. "It's so…the altitude, the air's thin."

He studied her, then nodded vaguely. "Sure," he said, then turned and spoke to her over his shoulder. "It's only ten feet or so, then we can cut into the forest. There's less snow in there and it's easier to walk."

She followed him, keeping her eyes on her footing, and all but pressing her left arm against the bank. "Here," he said and she looked up to see that the bank didn't actually go very high.

They were at a parting in the forest, and when she stepped into it to follow Duncan, she knew he was right. The snow in the shelter was thin and doable. And the light was softly diffused. Even the air felt strangely warmer here.

When she spoke, her voice echoed softly around them. "How did you find this?"

"I was just exploring one day and then I found out where it lead to."

"Which is?"

"The bird's-eye view I was talking about," he said. "Over there."

He motioned to a stream of light filtering through the trees and headed toward it. She went after him, through the foot-deep snow, the ground feeling spongy with each step. Then he stopped, waited for her and stepped out of the trees.

She followed and stopped, amazed at the view. "Wow," she gasped as she stepped onto a high promontory that jutted out of the forest and seemed to hang out in space. She got within two feet of the edge and couldn't go farther, but she didn't have to.

Spread out below, white and magical, was the inn, its dark buildings scattered on the grounds, the sweeping ski runs, and beyond that, the town of Silver Creek. She could make out the streets, the buildings, smoke curling into the sky from the chimneys. The mountains were off in the distance and everything was lost in a soft haze.

The resort was huge, incredibly expansive, shrouded in the beauty of the snow. Each cabin seemed private, positioned for the privacy that the rich and famous always claim to seek. The people near the lifts looked like black specks. But she could hardly take it all in.

Lauren felt a sudden urgency to get out of there, to return to town. She could barely breathe between the fresh air and Duncan's presence. Without thinking, she turned quickly and, for a split second, the world seemed to spin in front of her. She pushed back, away from the edge, and the next thing she knew, she was falling face down in the snow.

Embarrassed, she quickly shoved herself up, sputtering, awkwardly getting to her feet. She swiped at her eyes, knocking off her hood, and realized that she'd gone sideways, toward the trees into a drift by the massive trunk of a towering pine. The next thing she saw was Duncan standing right in front of her.

"What on earth happened?" he asked.

I looked at you, she thought but didn't say. Instead, she said, "I moved too fast, and the…the altitude, the air's so thin…" Her words faded when she realized he was smiling at her. No, he was almost laughing at her. "You think this is funny?" she asked, holding her arms out to her sides.

"You spun around, and made a perfect swan dive into the nearest snowbank," he murmured as he came closer. "But I don't think I should admit that it was amusing, should I?"

His deep voice echoed in the stillness, and all she could see was that smile, and the way it filled his dark eyes. Unnerved to say the least, and in an attempt to ease the tension between them, Lauren grabbed a handful of snow and was about to throw it at Duncan when he lunged for her.

He caught her hand with his and pulled her forward, against him, pinning her hand with the snow between his chest and hers. "Oh, no, you don't," he rasped.

The snow was painfully cold in her hands. "I wasn't going to do anything," she gasped, barely able to lift her head and look into his dark eyes. "Trust me."

"Trust you?" he asked, his breath brushing her wet face. "I don't trust anyone."

Chapter Twelve

Lauren wasn't stunned by Duncan's words, but knew there was no real reason to trust her. "I won't hurt you," she breathed. She didn't want to hurt Duncan. But to ask him to trust her was ludicrous.

"Okay, I trust you," he said, and although she knew he meant it only when it came to this moment, she felt sick. She hated lying.

She couldn't do this and pulled back, letting the melting snow fall from her freezing hand. "Okay," she said, then turned away from him. "Now, I have to get back."

She started walking toward the forested area and heard him follow. She moved through the thick trees, following the same path as before.

The walk was awkward, not only because of the slippery surface but thanks to the guilt that had welled up inside her. She kept going and was practically running by the time she hit the driveway. Once she reached the SUV, she was breathing hard and shivering from the dampness on her face and clothes.

She reached for the door handle and tugged, but it didn't give. Duncan covered her hand with his to stop her. "What's going on?"

"I've had enough fresh air," she murmured, pulling her hand away from the contact. Then she made herself turn and form what she hoped was a believably happy smile. "And I've got to go to work."

"Sure," he murmured.

She inclined her head toward the door. "Can you unlock this for me? It's freezing."

His eyes were narrowed on her. "I left the keys in the cabin," he said.

She couldn't stop a spontaneous shiver. "Then, could you get them, please?"

He turned and she watched him head back to the cabin, take the stairs in one long stride, then open the door and disappear inside. Once he was gone, she exhaled a breath she hadn't realized she'd been holding. Trust her? She knew right then that she'd meant it when she'd said it. It hadn't been a ploy. And she almost wished it had been.

She shivered violently, cold seeping into her being. From the very beginning she'd been on edge around Duncan, so very close to falling into a place she shouldn't. Then he'd told her about his life, about his reasons for what he'd done, and everything had changed. Duncan Bishop had turned out to be the moral person, and now she was anything but. She'd lied, manipulated and did it all in the name of her job, a job she really needed, and a bonus she'd do just about anything to get. And she wondered where her line would be drawn. Where would she stop and refuse to cross? Or would she?

Now she understood what he'd done, why he'd left, and couldn't argue with it. In fact, for him to walk away from all that money and power on principle was incredible. The thing was, she'd known how different he was from his father from the moment she'd met him. Looking into his dark eyes, listening to the sound of his voice, she'd known.

Even before he'd kissed her that first time she'd been affected merely by his presence. If she let herself, she could do more than care about Duncan Bishop.

Once she was back in town, she'd call Vern and tell him everything. Well, almost everything. Then she'd let him decide what to do, because she couldn't. And besides, it was his agency, his case. It was just her assignment.

She stomped from foot to foot trying to fight off the bone-chilling cold. As another shiver ran through her, she started for the cabin.

Once inside, Lauren found Duncan rifling through the drawers in the kitchen. She started to say something, but ended up gasping when she felt a burning in her hand. He turned as she tried to warm up. "What's going on?" she asked.

"I'm looking for the keys," he said.

"What?" she asked, starting to shiver.

His face was set in a dark frown. "I can't find the keys. I brought them in, but…" He undid his jacket and patted the pockets of his jeans. "Damn," he muttered.

"D-don't you…?" She was barely able to get out the

words when she started to shake all over. "An extra…a key somewhere?"

He looked at her again, and asked, "Are you okay?"

"Just…find the keys," she muttered. It was warm in the cabin and she should have been fine, but she couldn't stop shaking and her hand hurt terribly.

Duncan crossed to her and watched as she rubbed her sore hand. "What's wrong with your hand?"

"Snow, I…it's the one that I was holding the snow in, and it hurts," she said. She flexed it in front of her and saw how red it was. "It'll be okay."

"And you're shaking."

"I'm cold," she said.

He touched her again, on her jacket sleeve this time. "And you're wet. You need to get that jacket off and warm up while I look for the keys."

It sounded like a good idea, but she couldn't have un-done her jacket to save her life just then. Her hand hurt and she was shaking so hard, her teeth would have clat-tered if she hadn't kept her jaw tightly clenched. As if he could read her mind, Duncan unbuttoned her jacket and removed it. Lauren then made her way to the sofa that faced the fire and sank down onto the warm cush-ions.

Duncan came over and crouched down in front of her. Without saying a word, he took off her boots, then put them on the raised hearth. He took the time to put a couple more logs on the fire, waited for the flames to lick up around them, then turned back to her. "You sit there and I'll find the keys," he said.

She sat on the edge of the cushions, hugging herself,

trying to ignore the pain in her hand while she watched Duncan move around the cabin. As the fire grew, her trembling lessened and the pain in her hand eased. She saw Duncan take off his jacket, recheck the pockets, then lay it beside hers on the chair. He went to the bedroom area, then back to the kitchen, pulling open the cupboards this time.

When he returned to the sofa, he looked puzzled. "They have to be here. I didn't take them up to the lookout point." He frowned. "God, I hope I didn't. I don't remember having them up there."

"I didn't see them," she said.

"Feeling any better?" he asked.

She nodded. "Yes, I think so."

He studied her openly for a nerve-racking moment before touching her cheek. His heat seeped into her in a way the heat from the fire never could. She closed her eyes, almost unable to take in the sensations of his touch and certainly not able to meet his gaze. His fingers were gentle on her cheek, then moved slowly down until he was cupping her chin. "Too bad we don't have more time," he murmured.

She sighed and opened her eyes. He was still there, still touching her, his breath mingling with hers. She wanted more time with Duncan, time spent being honest and exploring whatever was going on between them. But this definitely wasn't it. Maybe when this was over, when everything was settled, she could talk to him, be honest with him, admit what she'd done and why. Maybe he'd understand.

"Not now," she breathed. Later.

"Yeah, find the keys," he whispered, and his hand lifted to brush the damp hair at her temples. "I can't tempt you to play hooky from work today?"

He could tempt her to do just about anything, she admitted to herself. "No, I have to get back."

"Too bad." His fingers trailed to her cheek, lingering there seductively. "I've told you I wanted to get to know you and I meant it. I want to know everything about you."

She sighed and sank back in the couch, breaking the contact. "There's nothing to know." The lie almost choked her.

He sat so close that his thigh pressed against hers. "Let me be the judge of that."

"No, let's find the keys," she said and started to get up to help him look. But he stopped her by placing a hand on her shoulder.

"I think I need to retrace our way to the lookout site, and see if I dropped them or something." His touch on her was light but compelling.

She sank back into the cushions with a sigh. "Can't we call someone?"

"No, I'll find them. The signal for cell phones isn't very strong." He let go of her. "I'll find the keys, don't worry about it."

But he didn't get up. He was watching her, and she was staring at the fire. "What?" she finally asked.

"I was just thinking what I know about you. You can't handle laced punch. You work hard. You're a pool shark, and you chew on your bottom lip whenever you're nervous."

She'd been doing that, but stopped immediately. "You don't—"

"No, I don't. I don't know how you'd act if you had to eat one of Annie's muffins, or how you really feel about me being a Bishop and what I've done."

Lauren wished she could tell him how very different he was from his father, that whatever "being a Bishop" meant, he was the one without the fatal flaws, unlike his father. That she wished she'd have had the courage to do the same thing he'd done, if she'd been in his situation. "I doesn't matter what I think," she said.

"Just tell me what's your favorite color, before I go on the great key hunt?"

She rested her head on the back of the couch and turned to look at him. The light in the cabin wasn't bright and his features seemed somewhat blurred, which was okay. She didn't want to see him too clearly. "Yellow, I guess."

"Favorite flower?"

She closed her eyes, trying to make things easier by not looking at him. "Roses, yellow roses."

"Favorite holiday?"

"Christmas."

"Favorite food?"

"I don't know. Something chocolate, I guess."

"Favorite time of day?"

"Twilight."

"Favorite city?"

She almost said Silver Creek, but it couldn't be. She didn't know the place any more than she really knew Duncan. Flexing her sore hand on the damp denim of her jeans, she said, "San Francisco, high up, overlooking the bay."

"Favorite book?"

She sighed. *"Pride and Prejudice."*

"Favorite song?"

"Any of the old standards."

"Which one specifically?"

"Maybe, 'The Very Thought of You.'" She bit her lip. No, not that one. She opened her eyes and stared at the ceiling. "I don't really know," she said, sitting up. "Sorry."

"One last question?"

"No," she said. Enough was enough. But he touched her shoulder with his hand again, and she knew she'd answer him.

"You're a mystery to me. I don't know where you're coming from. I don't know what this is all about. And I want to know."

She didn't move as his hand shifted from her shoulder to the nape of her neck. He brushed at her hair, skimming over her skin, and she held her breath, unable to look away from him. He was a large man, and right now, he filled her world. He did it so easily, so very easily, that she could wind up falling in love with him if she wasn't careful.

She looked at her hands and it was all she could do to whisper, "Duncan, I don't want to play this game anymore."

His hand cupped her chin, bringing her head up so she had to look at him. "I'm not playing a game," he said roughly, and leaned toward her. The minute his mouth found hers, she knew the games were over.

She opened her lips, inviting him to invade her, and then twisted around so she could circle his neck with her arms. She wanted him. It was that simple. Basic and intense. She wanted him more than she'd wanted anyone in her whole life.

Lacing her fingers in his hair, she arched toward him, aching to feel him against her. His mouth seared hers, exploring, tasting. His hands moved down her back, spanning her waist and lifting her up in one deft movement so that she was straddling him, arching back, exposing her throat to his kisses. His hands were on her, cupping her breasts through her top, then worked their way under the material and found the lace of her bra.

Lauren moaned softly when he managed to push aside the flimsy material and find her nipple, teasing it between his thumb and forefinger, sending waves of pleasure through her. He tugged at her sweater, slipping it off of her in one motion as she raised her arms, and tossing it over his shoulder. His fingers played with the clasp on her bra, and in a moment that was gone, too.

She gasped when his lips found the place his fingers had teased seconds earlier. He tugged at her nipple and shards of ecstasy shot through her, shaking her. Desperate to feel him, to have skin against skin, she tugged at his T-shirt, pulling it free of his jeans, pushing her hands under the soft cotton, feeling the sleek skin of his chest.

His hands were at her waist again, lifting her slightly, letting her feel the hardness of his desire. His lips buried in her neck, searing her skin with his kisses, finding her breast again. "Oh," she gasped, shaking, but it had nothing to do with the cold this time and everything to do with the man touching her.

"I want you," he whispered as he eased back, lifting his hands to frame her face.

She opened her eyes and knew without a doubt that she wanted him, too. Driven to feel more, to experience more, she was desperate for his touch. No, no, she couldn't do this. She suddenly felt naked and embarrassed, and twisted awkwardly to get away from him to get to her feet. She grabbed her sweater, her hands shaking so hard she could barely get her arms in the sleeves.

"I can't do this," she breathed as she pulled it down over her. Then she saw her bra on the couch and reached for it. She looked around the cabin, anywhere but at Duncan still sitting on the couch watching her. "The keys," she muttered. "The damn keys, the keys, the keys." She was feeling frantic, skittering her eyes over the place, but she couldn't see any keys.

"Hey, it's okay. I'm not pushing anything," he said as he stood, his arm brushing hers as he got to his feet.

She all but jumped out of her skin, turned to him, and then wished she hadn't. It wasn't okay at all. His dark eyes were on her and he didn't make a move to hide the evidence of his arousal. Thankfully, she could hide her own desire, even if it felt like a knot inside her. "Where are the keys?" she asked, her voice high and tight and the discarded bra being crushed in her hand.

He took his time tucking his T-shirt back into his jeans. "If I knew that—" he drawled with annoying composure as he re-buttoned his Levi's "—I'd have them, wouldn't I?"

And none of this would have happened. She turned from him and grabbed her jacket. She put it on, pushed the bra in a pocket, then put on her boots. She'd walk to find the keys if she had to, but as she looked up from fastening her last boot, she saw Duncan had his jacket on and was tugging his watch cap down.

"I'll be back," he murmured and headed for the door.

As soon as he opened the door, she looked away, and that's when she saw a glint of silver in the stack of logs by the fire. Looking more closely she saw the keys half-hidden in a space under the bottom log. "I found them," she called right before the door closed.

He stopped and turned. "What?"

"The keys. They were under the wood on the fire-place." She held up the key ring with the remote for him to see. "You must have dropped them when you made the fire."

He looked at them, but didn't take them. "Get the car started while I lock up in here."

When he came toward her, she moved aside, and then headed for the SUV. The sky was getting darker, blotting out a good share of the sun now, and a wind was starting to pick up. By the time she got in and started the engine, Duncan was hurrying toward the SUV.

He got in, shutting the door, then snapped on his seat belt. Lauren thought he was going to touch her again and she jerked back, embarrassed when he simply gripped the side of her seat to twist and look over his shoulder to back the SUV down the driveway.

She knew he saw her flinch, and her hands clenched in her lap when he murmured, "I'll get you back in time for work."

Duncan drove staring straight ahead, saying nothing, a muscle working in his jaw and his hands flexing on the steering wheel. By the time they were near the hotel, she was almost sick from nerves. "I'm really sorry," she finally blurted out.

"You tend to apologize a lot, don't you?" he said without looking at her. "I should be the one apologizing again."

She watched him slow down for the traffic. "No, I'm the one who…" She bit her lip. "Things just got out of hand."

When he reached the hotel he swung into the side parking area. The slot where her car had been was filled by a Mercedes sedan—black, sleek and very expensive.

"Yeah, they did," he finally said as he pulled into a parking spot. He didn't shut off the engine, but instead turned to face her, his left hand still resting on top of the steering wheel. Dark eyes were narrowed and there wasn't a smile at his lips anymore. "I didn't mean to push you."

"It wasn't that," she said. "It just can't happen."

His expression grew tighter. "Why?"

The single word was there, hanging between them, and totally unanswerable right now. "I can't explain now," she said, then heard herself finish. "Later."

"Is that a promise?" he asked.

She nodded. "Yes, I promise." She reached for the

door handle and got out, then hurried to the hotel and went inside without looking back.

She heard voices in the lobby and tried to be quiet, hoping to get through without being noticed. A middle-aged couple sat nibbling on muffins at a table that Annie had set up by the front window. She kept walking and reached the stairs without anyone addressing her. Halfway up the stairs, she heard footsteps behind her. When she got to the second floor, she heard Annie call out, "Hey, you two! Hold up."

Lauren turned to see Duncan stepping past her and into the hallway. Annie was right behind him. Dressed all in blue, she said, "I thought that was the two of you coming in. Just back from work, Lauren?"

"I'm going to work soon," Lauren said. "And I need to get a move on or I'm going to be late."

But Annie wasn't done chatting yet. "Lauren, I've got a message for you from Rollie."

Lauren stopped and turned. "Oh, what is it?"

Annie unfolded a piece of paper and read, "Fuel pump can be here tomorrow. Cost installed two hundred and ten dollars. Also needs filter and one section of fuel line. Price out the door, an even three hundred dollars." Annie looked at her. "He needs to know by two o'clock if that's okay."

"Thanks," she said. "I'll call him."

"I'm going down that way to get some supplies," Annie said. "Do you want me to stop by and give him a message for you?"

"I'd appreciate it. Could you tell him to go ahead and get it done as quickly as he can."

"No problem," Annie said and turned to go back downstairs with a wave.

It was just Lauren and Duncan now. He came toward her and stood there until she looked up at him. "That promise of yours?" he asked in a low voice.

She stared at him. "Yes."

"I'm going to hold you to it," he said, then turned and headed for his room.

Chapter Thirteen

Lauren had made a promise and she meant to keep it. But she couldn't do anything until she talked to Vern. And Vern was gone for two days on a "mini vacation" with his wife. If he'd told her before about it, she hadn't taken it in. Now she had to wait for two days to talk to him, two days before she could keep her promise to Duncan.

She went into work that afternoon, kept busy and waited. Duncan was nowhere to be seen, and part of her was thankful she didn't have to be around him for now. But the other part of her looked for him every time the door opened. And when it wasn't him coming into the diner, she was disappointed. Then, a half hour before her shift ended, Duncan appeared.

She came out of the kitchen, heard chimes over the constant Christmas music and looked across at the door opening. Duncan strode in, snow clinging to his clothes, and he stopped to skim off his watch cap. When his dark eyes met hers, the impact of the connection made her stop in her tracks. Then he looked away and she took a breath before hurrying over to the table by the windows with an order.

Out of the corner of her eye Lauren watched Duncan head toward the office. She knew she'd been wanting to see him, but now that he was here, she wished he hadn't come. Being around him was too unsettling for her, too prone to make her remember hours ago when he'd touched her. She went back into the kitchen, stopped inside the door to take a few cleansing breaths and almost jumped out of her skin when Rusty spoke to her.

"Getting crazy out there?" he asked, and she turned to see him sitting at the small counter they used to do their paperwork.

Crazy? Absolutely. "It's busy," she murmured, then spoke to the cook. "Any baked potatoes yet?"

He shook his head. "Five minutes more."

She took another deep breath, then went back out into the restaurant. Occupying her time by checking on the tables in her station, refilling drinks and resetting the booths by the fireplace, she was surprised to see Duncan sitting alone in her station. There was no way to get out of going over there.

She braced herself, hoping against hope that he'd order something, eat and leave. She didn't know what to say. There was nothing she could say. She crossed to him, pad and pencil in hand. He held a menu he wasn't looking at; his jacket and hat were on the seat beside him.

"I didn't think you were coming in today," she said.

"Neither did I," he murmured.

"You...you're eating?"

"That's the plan."

How did you make small talk with a man you'd almost made love with hours ago? A man whom you could still feel on your skin? It didn't help when his dark eyes dropped lower, skimming over her breasts, then made their way back to her face. And although she'd put on a bra before work, Lauren was starting to feel naked again. She touched her tongue to her lips, then managed to ask, "Okay, what will it be?"

His answer was direct and simple. "Chili, corn bread and coffee."

She wrote, trying to ignore images flashing through her mind—sitting on his lap, his hands on her breasts, then his lips. "Is that it?" she asked, staring at her pad and not at him.

"When are you done here?" he asked.

She met his gaze. The question was simple, but the look in his eyes wasn't. "I'm not sure." She pushed the pencil into her apron, but held tightly to the order pad. "Anything else?"

He shook his head, and she walked away quickly, feeling his eyes on her. After placing his order, Lauren decided all she could do was her job. So she picked up the coffeepot and went back out to the dining room.

Once she'd filled his mug, she attempted to walk away. But he stopped her by saying her name.

"Lauren?"

"Cream?" she asked.

"No, I want to talk to you," he said, and she held tightly to the handle of the hot coffeepot.

"I'm busy," she said, knowing how abrupt and rude her words sounded even as she headed back into the kitchen.

She had to get bread baskets for tables two and five. She put them together quickly, got small dishes of butter and put them in the baskets with the rolls, then turned to take them to the customers. But Duncan was coming into the kitchen, blocking her exit.

"I know you're busy," he said. "But I wanted to talk, and I wondered if we could get together once you're off? It's important."

"I can't. I'm tired and I just want to get some rest after work." She wanted nothing more than just to tell him the truth, to get it over with, but she couldn't. Instead, she held up the bread baskets and said, "I need to get these out while they're hot."

She'd barely finished the sentence before he'd turned and left. Just like that. The door was swinging shut after him. She closed her eyes for a moment, then went through the door, and couldn't stop herself from looking over at Duncan's table. When she saw it was empty, she exhaled and crossed to deliver the bread.

Duncan went back into the office, closed the door and muttered an oath as he punched one hand into the palm of the other. Damn it, he hated this. He hated not knowing what was going on. He hated feeling out of control. He hated being frustrated and edgy and he hated the fact he'd opened up to her only to have her shut him out. Had she had a bad relationship? A bad marriage?

Something had made her stop suddenly when they'd

been about to make love. She'd wanted him. He knew that. And she wasn't being coy, telling him they needed more time to get to know each other. He could have bought that. They'd barely known each other, even though he felt as if she'd been in his world forever. He wasn't going to push himself on her. He'd never been like that. No meant no. But there was something she wasn't telling him. He could have sworn he saw fear in her eyes. "I can't" was all she'd said. "I can't."

He closed his eyes and was almost overwhelmed by images of Lauren. The way she'd arched toward him, the soft gasps, the taste of her, the feel of her skin under his hands. Her breasts naked, full and seductive, the nipples tightened into hard nubs. He stopped those thoughts right there. Just thinking about her was making his body start to respond, and that wouldn't help anything.

Besides, it wasn't that he had to have her physically, although he wanted her more than he'd ever wanted another woman. But he wanted her, period. He wanted to know her, to understand her, simply to love her. Love. He didn't know where that feeling came from, or even what it would be like to love another person. But whatever this was with Lauren was probably as close as he'd ever gotten to the real thing.

He opened his eyes to the small office and saw the tall filing cabinets along the wall. Five drawers in one, and two of them were for employee records—applications, tax forms, verifying documentation for hiring. He crossed to it, pulled out the top drawer that ran *A* through *M,* fingering through the tabs until he reached the one labeled Carter, Lauren.

There wasn't much in it. Just an application that
barely filled out and a plain sheet of paper filled
feminine handwriting. The application contained
name, Lauren Joy Carter, and a birth date of Ju
Twenty-seven years old. Her social security num
But no address.

He picked up the other sheet and read, "Refere
Lauren Carter."

He scanned the references. Restaurants he'd n
heard of, two in Arizona, one in Oregon and the las
in California. That was the only one with a phone n
ber and the address simply read Brentwood, Califo
The Wind Chimes. He turned to the desk, reache
the phone and put in the number.

It rang twice before a perky voice said, "The V
Chimes Restaurant. How may I help you?"

"Can I speak with your manager?"

"You're speaking with the manager," the voice

"I'm checking on a reference for one of your
employees."

"Oh, yes, certainly. Where are you calling from

"Rusty's Diner, in Silver Creek, Nevada."

"Who were you inquiring about?"

"Lauren Carter."

She never missed a beat. "Oh, yes, of course.
Carter worked here for a while." She gave him dates
matched the handwritten notes on the paper. "Exce
waitress. Good with people. Trustworthy. A
worker."

He almost asked if she walked on water. "Why
she leave?"

"Personal reasons," the woman said, suddenly vague.

"Family problems?"

"I couldn't say."

He asked the standard question a prospective employer would ask. "Would you hire her again?"

"Absolutely," she said with conviction.

"Thank you," he said and hung up.

"Excuse me?"

He turned to see Lauren standing in the doorway. He hadn't even heard the door open.

"Are you finished working?"

"No, I just wanted to let you know your food's ready."

Wearing jeans, an apron and little to no makeup, she was still breathtaking. He inhaled, caught that scent that he associated with her, a freshness, flowers maybe, something more. Her shirt was a thin cotton, and he found himself wondering if she was wearing a bra now.

He was acting like a damn teenager. "Thanks for letting me know," he said. Then she left as quietly as she'd appeared.

He'd had enough. Coming in here had been a bad idea. He should have stayed at the cabin. After dropping Lauren at the hotel, Duncan had gone back there to be alone, to try to figure things out. He'd thought about what she'd said in regards to his father. About going back. And he'd thought about her. That was what had driven him to come back tonight. Images and thoughts and frustration.

Everything seemed backward and upside down. Nothing about his relationship with Lauren made sense or fit the patterns of any other relationships he'd ever had. But then again, he'd never met Lauren before, either, and he'd never even thought about loving a woman. Love hadn't been necessary, but suddenly it was hovering around the fringes of his life.

Love? He'd joked about the *L* word, was sure it didn't exist, that it was a romantic notion for people to hang their hearts on. But he wasn't laughing now. The thought made him leave the office and return to the dining room. His food was on the table, but Lauren was nowhere in sight. After leaving money to cover the bill, Duncan grabbed his jacket and hat and headed outside into the snowy night.

He headed north and didn't stop walking until he reached the Briar. Inside the place was practically empty.

He nodded to Pudge, slid onto a stool at the bar, and asked for a whiskey straight up. Love? He took the drink when Pudge brought it, drained half of it, then set the glass on the polished bar.

"Hey, I'm sorry about that thing with your girlfriend," Pudge said, swiping a rag on the bar top. "Never thought she wouldn't know about the booze in the punch."

Duncan tossed off the rest of his whiskey and motioned for a refill before he answered. "You should warn people about its effects," he said. "Maybe hang a sign, and avoid lawsuits or worse."

The man didn't take offense. "Yeah, good idea" was all he said.

Duncan lifted the glass again, and Pudge wandered

down to the other end of the bar to polish glasses and talk to the only other person sitting there. Duncan stared at his drink, then set it down on the bar top. He didn't need to get drunk. He needed to think, to figure out what he was going to do now.

When Pudge came to check on his drink, Duncan said, "I've got a question and was hoping maybe you'd have some answers."

"HEY, LAUREN," RUSTY CALLED as he came into the kitchen where she sat tallying a bill at the small desk. "Table three's ready for their bill, and there's a customer at table seven. I put in his ticket for coffee, black, a BLT on whole wheat, no toast and home fries. Get his coffee out to him, and smile for him, okay? He's a good guy."

"He's a friend?" she asked as she found table three's bill and checked it.

"Josh? Yeah, I've known him since he was in diapers. Me and his old man, Sheriff Pierce, have been friends for years and years. Now Josh is helping out at the sheriff's office, at least until his dad's better."

She slipped the bill into her apron pocket, crossed to pour the coffee and said, "I'll get it out to him."

He glanced at the clock. "You're off in five minutes. Just get him going, and Arlene can take over for you."

"Sure," she said and took the coffee out. She glanced at Duncan's table. He was gone. She took the sheriff his coffee, smiled for the man, then went back to Duncan's table. His food was untouched, and two ten-dollar bills lay by the plate. A hundred percent tip. She grabbed the money, pushed it into her pocket and crossed to give table three their bill. Five minutes later, she was in the office getting her jacket when something caught her attention.

On top of the filing cabinet lay an open folder. She immediately recognized her own handwriting. It was then she remembered Duncan in here earlier, on the phone.

On impulse, she lifted the phone and hit the redial button. She waited as it rang twice, then a voice answered, "The Wind Chimes Restaurant. How can I help you?"

"Beth?"

The woman was silent, then said, "You must have the wrong number."

"No, it's me, Lauren. Who called about me?"

"A man, said he was from Rusty's Diner in Silver Creek, Nevada." She laughed softly. "Not to worry, I gave you a glowing reference."

Duncan had checked on her. It made sense. She was being mysterious with him, off-putting, and he thought he could find out something about her. Yes, it made sense, but it bothered her, too. "Thanks for covering for me."

"It's my job," Beth said and hung up.

Lauren left the file where she found it and put on her jacket. Stepping out into the street, Lauren knew the temperature had dropped. She headed back to the hotel. When she pushed her hand into her pocket, she felt her bra still in there. She'd been crazy to let things go that far. Walking faster, she reached the spot where the car had almost hit her. Duncan had saved her life. Then he'd told her that crazy thing about being responsible for her. She was responsible for herself and what she did. No one else.

Pausing to check the traffic before crossing to the hotel, Lauren stopped when she saw Duncan heading through the front door of the hotel. He was alone. She watched him cross the lobby to talk to Annie at the front desk. Clearly he was in no hurry to move on. There was no way she was going in there now. She just couldn't face him.

She looked farther up the street, then crossed and headed north. She really didn't know where she was going until she saw the sign for the Briar.

It was warm when she stepped inside, the air smelling of wood smoke. Pudge stood behind the bar and when he saw her, he smiled and came over to her.

"Hey, darling," he said with what looked like a sheepish smile. "I owe you a big apology about that punch. Should've warned you. I just assumed everyone knew old Pudge spiked that stuff." He pointed to a handwritten sign on the mirror behind the bar. "I just put that up." In bright red, it said Beware of Holiday Punch! It Contains Alcohol.

She appreciated the apology. "I'll know enough to ask what's in punch when I get it next time," she said.

"That'd be real smart," he said. "Bar or table for you?"

"Table," she said, unbuttoning her jacket.

He took her to a small table by the fireplace, and while she settled in a chair facing the fire, he asked,

"What can I get you?" Before she could answer, he said, "And if you want punch, I'll do it without the punch." He grinned at his own joke. "Punchless punch."

"Coffee would be just fine," she said. "Black."

"You got it, darling." He headed back toward the bar while she slipped off her jacket and put it over the back of her chair. Then he was back with the coffee, setting it in front of her along with a basket of pretzels. As she cradled the mug between her hands, Pudge pulled out the chair facing her, turned it around and straddled it. He rested his chin on his hands on the chair back. "You're looking as confused as Duncan was when he was in here."

"When was he here?" she asked.

"A bit ago. He looked as if he had the weight of the world on his shoulders, and asked me a few questions."

"Such as?"

"Such as, did I understand women?" He laughed at that. "Me? Married four times, and divorced as many?" He shook his head. "Hell, a good P.I. couldn't answer those questions he had. They could find out what people did, but not why. Who in the hell knows why anyone does anything?" The door opened and a party of six men came in, their voices raised and obviously having a good time. "Gotta go," Pudge said and stood, turning the chair back to its original station.

As he walked away, something he had said stuck with her about a P.I. *They could find out what people did, but not why.* She could do that, find out what someone did. She sipped the coffee, letting the soothing liquid slide down her throat. They could even find out what a man like D. R. Bishop did. Then something Duncan had said wove its way into her thoughts. He hadn't known about his father's "romantic" history, and that he might even have a brother or sister out there somewhere.

She put the coffee down. All she knew about D.R. was his actions in the business world and what little she'd learned from her one conversation with him. He'd been married to Duncan's mother, but the man had an ego the size of Texas. And women were drawn to men like that. Power and wealth were aphrodisiacs. And who knew what D.R. had done in the past?

She wished she'd brought her cell phone, but a pay phone was the next best thing, and she saw one back by the pool tables. Dialing the agency, she looked at her watch. It was seven now, and it was an hour earlier in Los Angeles. Maybe someone would be there. But it rang four times, then flipped over to the answering service. She almost hung up, then thought better of it.

"Hi, this is Lauren Carter. I work for the agency. I need you to ring an extension for me." She gave the person the number for Vern's assistant, Madge Brenner. Lauren thought that of all the operatives, Madge was the one most likely still to be hanging around the offices. And she was right.

"Madge Brenner."

"Madge, it's Lauren." There was small talk, but Lauren hurried past it. "I need you to do something for me."

Madge was as unlikely an operative as you'd find, middle-aged, with the face of a kindly aunt. She was a housewife who had wanted to get out of the house after her kids had grown, and had turned out to be one of the best operatives in the agency. "Sure thing, kiddo. What's needed?"

"Do you know if we did a background check on D. R. Bishop?"

"I'll look." Lauren heard the keys of a computer keyboard clicking, then Madge was back. "No, just did them for him on other people."

"Okay, that's what I need. A background check. But I don't want his business past in it, just his personal history."

"What are you looking for?"

"Anything, but give special attention to his relationships, and anything that came out of them."

"How do you want it when I have it ready?"

"Call in to my cell phone. It works off and on up here, so if it goes to voice mail, leave a message and I'll call you back."

"You've got it."

She hung up, then went back to her table. The coffee was tepid now and unappetizing, but she was ready to leave anyway. She put on her jacket, left the money for the coffee and headed to the door, calling to Pudge at the bar, "Thanks for everything."

"You have a great night, darling."

Hurrying outside into the frigid evening, Lauren headed back to the hotel through the falling snow. She looked in the front window to make sure Duncan wasn't still in the lobby, then made her way to the stairs and went up.

Her footsteps echoed as she climbed. At the second floor, she noticed a light coming from Duncan's room. Making her way to her own room, Lauren hoped she wouldn't run into Duncan again until she'd talked to Madge. But that hope was dashed when just as she was about to unlock her door, she sensed him behind her. She turned, and he was stepping up into the hallway. No jacket, no hat, no boots. Just jeans, a T-shirt and bare feet. And she knew in that second that she loved him. It wasn't a question. It wasn't a maybe. It was a fact.

And he couldn't be here. He couldn't be coming closer. He couldn't be stopping in front of her and he couldn't be saying, "I have to talk to you."

Chapter Fourteen

Duncan had been in his room since returning from Rusty's, doing nothing but listening for someone coming up the stairs. Linus had come and gone. Annie had come up, gone to the third floor, then went back down. A couple at the end of the hall had left. Finally, he'd heard Lauren. He'd opened his door just as she'd disappeared up the next flight of stairs and he'd followed her, not bothering to put on shoes. There was an urgency in him, and he wasn't sure where it came from, but it made it impossible for him not to go after her.

Somewhere between leaving the Briar and getting back to the hotel, he'd decided that he didn't have to know about what was in Lauren's past. All he needed to know was she was here and he was here. That's all that mattered. Being in the same place in the world at the same time as her. The time they'd known each other didn't matter. A day, a week, a year. He didn't think time would make what he was feeling any more real.

He caught up to her as she was opening the door to her room, then she turned, and he could see that same fear in her eyes that had been there before. But she didn't go in and slam the door. That was a relief. She held on to the door handle, watching him, nibbling on her bottom lip. She looked as nervous as he felt right then, and he told her he needed to talk to her.

She tipped her head slightly to look up at him and finally said in a mere whisper, "I told you I was tired."

"Me, too," he admitted on an exhale. That was the truth. He was tired of being alone, being in a world that he never felt he belonged in, until he looked into lavender eyes, a delicately beautiful face framed by feathery auburn hair, and heard a voice that seeped into his soul. "I've done a lot of thinking. Mostly in circles, but a few things filtered through."

She didn't ask him what things or tell him that he had to go. Instead, she simply sighed, "Oh, Duncan," as if she couldn't take it anymore, either.

He said the things he'd only thought to himself up until that moment. "I don't care about your past, what you were or what happened, but I care about you, and being here with you. Right here. In this spot." He took a shuddering breath. "I've always needed answers, always held out for them, but right now, that's not what I need."

She closed her eyes for a moment, then looked at him again, her expression slightly shadowed by the dim overhead lights. But the impact of her gaze shook him. Almost as much as her next words did. "What do you need?"

They were little more than a whisper, but they opened his world to absolute truth. "You," he breathed. "You."

He moved closer to her, reaching out, framing her face with his hands, and he could feel his own unsteadiness echoing in her. She was shaking and he felt her take a shuddering breath.

"You don't know me," she breathed. "You don't—"

"Yes, I do." And he cut off any talking by covering her lips with his.

The moment he felt her softness and her heat, he was lost. Saying he wanted her was such an inadequate way to describe what he felt then. He needed her, had to be with her. He couldn't walk away, couldn't stop tasting her and needing to draw her closer to him than was humanly possible. He wanted to be with her, to be in her and to be part of her. He wanted her with a heart that ached and a soul that had to have her to be whole.

If she'd drawn back, if she'd stopped him in any way, he would have left. He couldn't have done otherwise, but, thankfully, she didn't pull away, didn't ask him to stop. Instead, she arched into him, her arms lifting to circle his neck, her mouth opening, and he lifted her into his arms. Her legs wrapped around his waist and he kicked open the door with his foot as he carried her into her room.

He reached blindly behind him, never stopping the kisses as he found the door and swung it shut, enclosing them in the tiny space. He carried her to the bed, dropping onto it, with her straddling him the way she had at the cabin. Her hands moved to frame his face, her lips trailing over him, kissing his eyes, then back to his mouth, their breath mingling together.

The earlier urgency took on a life of its own, and he

worked at getting her jacket off, then pushing it back and down, until it was free and he could toss it onto the floor. His lips moved from hers, to her throat, to a pulse that beat wildly there and he fumbled with the buttons on her shirt. But she took over, and the shirt was open, the cotton slipping off her shoulders, then her arms, then gone.

This time she undid the bra she was wearing, shrugging out of it, and her breasts were there for him, beautiful and full, the nipples already puckering and he tasted one, then the other, her soft moaning sounds almost animalistic. Her hands were on him, tugging at his shirt, freeing it from his waistband, then he lifted his arms and she pulled it over his head and off. Her hands were on his skin, the contact almost burning him, then she bent to him, and her mouth found his nipple, echoing his actions, but his groan was a shudder as ecstasy shot through him.

He was ready to explode and he didn't want to rush but he wanted to take his time, to enjoy every inch of her, to pleasure her and have her in a way he had never had a woman before. He twisted, turning on the bed, and they fell into the linen together, side by side. Her hands found the fastener on his Levi's, tugging to make the button pop open, then she tried to undo the zipper, but his swelling pressed against it so firmly that she couldn't get it to slide.

He moved back, hating the loss of contact, but needing to get rid of anything between them. He stood, quickly got the Levi's off, and while he did, she pushed her own jeans down, kicking them off the end of the bed, then she looked up at him. Her eyes were on him as he stepped out of his underwear, and he stood before her for a moment, speaking the words he had to say. "Are you sure?" he breathed in a rough whisper.

She looked at him, then at his face, and she held out her hands to him. "Yes."

Never had that word sounded so sweet. He went to her, lying with her, pulling her to him, running his hand over her bare back, then tucked his fingers in the waist of her panties. Slowly, he slid them down, then pushed them lower, letting her wiggle her feet out of them. Naked, they lay together, just feeling skin against skin, heat mingling with heat. Then she touched him. Her hand circled his hard heat, and any thoughts of taking it easy, of going slow, were lost.

He kissed her, devouring her, needing her with a single-mindedness that he'd never known. He splayed his hand on her stomach, lower, then lower again, and he found her center. He pressed his hand there and she rose toward him, pressing against his pressure, and when he moved on her, she gasped and arched up to him.

He shifted over her, bracing himself with a hand by her shoulders, then found her center with his strength, touching her, testing her, then slowly, he pushed into her and filled her. He looked down at her under him, her head back, her eyes closed, then they opened. The rich lavender was dazed with the same pleasure he was feeling. As he moved, she matched him, thrust for thrust, her hips rising to meet him, her legs going around him, pulling him even deeper.

She gasped, "Yes, oh, yes," and arched more and

more, her fingers digging into his shoulders, her legs tight, and the minute he knew he couldn't hold off any longer, he felt her shudder and gasp, and the release was complete. Together they called out, voices mingling, bodies becoming one, and in that instant, he knew what love was. He loved her.

They fell back to reality together, holding on to each other and he didn't leave her until he had to. They lay facing each other, his chin resting on the top of her head, his arm around her waist, her leg resting heavily on his thighs. He'd meant to talk. He'd told himself that's why he'd waited for her, watched for her, but he knew that was wrong. He'd been waiting for this moment. This was where he belonged.

He held her to him, closed his eyes and released a breath he felt he'd been holding all his life. Then he drifted into sleep, still holding her to him.

Lauren lay in the darkened room with Duncan as he held her and slept beside her for what could have been an eternity, or maybe just an hour. She didn't know. Time had no meaning for her right then. Her body was sated, but her heart ached. She buried her face in the sleek heat of his chest, feeling his heart against her cheek, listening to each steady beat, memorizing the moment to carry with her forever.

She'd never meant for this to happen, but she couldn't have wished it hadn't. She loved him. It was that simple, and that complicated. Loving him was the easy part. Being with him was just as easy, but the moment she'd have to explain was still ahead of them. She felt him stir, and wished he wouldn't waken now. Just a bit longer before she had to face what she'd done. Just a few more hours, even minutes.

But he shifted and she felt him press a kiss to her hair. She couldn't pretend anymore. "You're awake?" she whispered against his skin.

"Sort of." His voice sounded thick from sleep, a low rumble in his chest against her breast. He kissed her head again and sighed. "How about you?"

She shifted away from him a bit, lifting herself on one elbow to look down at him in the dim light. God, she loved him. She loved the way his eyes narrowed on her, the fullness of his bottom lip, the way his hair clung to his forehead. "I'm awake," she said.

He reached out and touched her shoulder, his finger trailing along her skin, making her breath catch in her chest and her stomach start to knot. She'd thought she'd had enough, that she was satisfied, but she knew in that moment that she'd never have enough of this man. She'd never be satisfied. She'd always want more and more. "Hmm," he said. "We're both awake. How convenient." And he smiled, a seductive expression that only made her want him more.

"Why did you come up here?" she made herself ask, steeling herself not to fall into his arms again.

His finger stilled on her, then shifted and his hand rested on the curve of her hip. "I wanted to tell you something."

She didn't want him to tell her anything else, not yet. "No, I need to—"

His hand lifted and he rested his forefinger on her lips. "No, I need to tell you something I figured out tonight." She would have gotten out of bed right then, put a barrier between them, anything so he wouldn't feel free to share things with her, but she couldn't. Breaking the contact was terrifying to her at that moment.

She reached for his hand, catching it in hers and tugging it to the spot between her breasts. "Rest for now," she said softly.

He exhaled, his breath brushing her skin with his warmth. "I heard what you said about my father and me, about going back and settling things."

She never expected him to say this, and she sat up abruptly, letting go of his hand. "What?"

He looked up at her, and it wasn't fair that he touched her again, cupping her breast and making her start to tremble. "You were right. I need to go back, do what I can, and if I can't do anything, at least I've tried instead of walking out." He raised enough to kiss her nipple, then sank back into the sheets, looking up at her, the shadow of a smile playing at the corners of his mouth. "Thank you," he said, then trailed his hand up to her shoulder, and to the nape of her neck where he cupped her, and gently pulled her down to him. "Thank you," he whispered against her lips, then kissed her.

Lauren was stunned, totally unprepared for what he'd told her. He was going to go back. He was doing it because he wanted to. She kissed him back. It was perfect. Perfect. He was doing what he wanted to do, and she knew that she was, too. She was loving him. She'd tell him, soon, but right then, all she wanted to do was love him. And she did.

She kissed him, while her hands trailed over his taut

stomach, down lower, finding him, and he was ready for her again. She reached up to kiss him, and he caught her by her waist and lifted her up and over onto him. She straddled him, and he lowered her down, entering her, filling her, and she all but collapsed on him. The sensations were almost unbearable, then he started to move and she gasped with pleasure. Higher and higher, the feelings built, and entangled with the feelings was the single thought that she loved him. She loved him.

And as they both climaxed, and she came back to reality, she lay on his chest, hearing his heart, and she began to cry silently. "Hey," he breathed, cupping her chin, making her look at his shadowed eyes. "Tell me what's wrong."

She drew out of his hold, closing her eyes so tightly colors exploded behind them. "Later," she whispered. "Later."

All he said was, "Okay," and he held her.

When Lauren woke, sunlight was coming in the single window, and she knew she was alone. She turned and Duncan was gone. The only trace he'd been there at all was the way the linen was tangled in the bed, a tenderness in her body and a piece of folded paper on the nightstand by the clock.

She reached for it and saw a feminine script on the top part. *Rollie said car will be ready tomorrow afternoon. Annie.* Under it, written in strong black letters: *Back soon. Will check on car. We'll talk. Promise. D.*

Promise. She folded the paper again and tossed it back on the nightstand. She'd made her own promise to him, and last night she'd made one to herself. To end this as quickly as possible. She'd been stunned when he'd told her he would go back. Now she just had to tell him about herself.

She sat up, the air slightly chilled, ready to shower and get dressed, then find Duncan. But before she could do any of that, her cell phone rang. She reached for it from the nightstand, checked the caller ID and opened it quickly. It was Madge.

She looked at the clock. It was early, barely eight here, so it couldn't be more then seven back in L.A. "Madge?"

"It's me," Madge said over the line. "Are you awake?"

"Yes."

"Good. I've got what you asked for."

She had to take a half second to focus. What she'd asked for? "Oh, yes, well, I'm not sure I need it now."

"Well, thanks," Madge said. "Here I have something spectacular and you're telling me you don't need it."

"Spectacular?" she asked, drawing her legs up to sit crossed-legged in the mussed bed.

"Okay, I'm exaggerating a bit, but it's interesting."

"What is it, Madge?"

"There are no kids running around because of the old man's affairs, but he had a brother who was two years older than him, named Warren. Poor guy died when he was twenty-eight, the day after his birthday, in a car accident caused by a drunk driver."

Lauren hadn't known about a younger brother. She'd concentrated on possible progeny, not siblings. "What about Warren?"

"There was just D.R. and Warren, and Warren never married."

"Well, this is interesting, but that's about it."

"You were thinking you could find another Bishop, take D.R.'s obsession with his son, transfer it to another family member and maybe get around his son having to come back."

"How did you—"

"Because, that's what I would have done if I'd run into a brick wall. And I thought you must have hit your brick wall."

Madge was good, very good. "I wish you'd found a little Bishop running around," she said, to give Duncan a choice.

"You didn't let me finish," Madge said quickly. "You haven't heard the good part. There was no marriage, but it seems that there was something left behind by Warren."

Lauren held the phone tightly. "What?"

"A son, born six months after his death. Warren's name's on the birth certificate as father, and the mother is a woman called Sheila Kennedy. David Bishop Kennedy is the boy's name."

"Yes!" she said with feeling. "Tell me about him."

"Thirty-nine, born in Palo Alto, raised there by his mother who never married. And the best part is that he's an attorney in San Francisco, a litigator with a reputation for taking no prisoners. One man I spoke to called him hell on wheels. I believe the man also called him a heartless bastard."

Another D.R.? "Thank you," Lauren said with feeling again. "You are a terrific investigator."

"From your lips to Vern's ears when raise time comes."

"I'll let him know how good you are," she said. "I couldn't have done all of this digging from here. Can you put this all together for me and I'll be back to get it in a day or two?"

"You've got it, Lauren," Madge said, then hung up.

Lauren had hoped for an errant offspring of D.R., but this was every bit as good. Another man who was a Bishop and who could fit in with the old man, take Duncan's place in the business and take the pressure off Duncan. She hadn't held much hope for it, but his one statement about brothers or sisters had been the thing to get this all started. Now she could offer this to D.R. as a solution.

She couldn't stay in the room a minute longer waiting for Duncan to come back. She'd get dressed and go and find him at Rollie's or Rusty's and tell him everything. She'd do it in a public place where she could keep her distance from him. In this room, she'd never get around to explaining anything.

She put on her robe, grabbed some towels and went barefoot down the stairs. She showered quickly and wished she'd brought fresh clothes with her. She hurried back to her room, and Duncan was there waiting. He was by the dresser, something in his hand, but all she saw was him. She could barely breathe.

"I'm glad you're back," she said, realizing that she'd missed him horribly. "You left early."

He shrugged. "I had things to do."

She had thought when he came back, she'd go to him, and touch him, make sure everything that had happened had been real. But she couldn't move and she felt awkward. "Did you see about the car?"

"It'll be done this afternoon."

Something was wrong. She swallowed hard, trying to focus, trying to figure out what was going on. Dropping her towels on the bed she turned back to him. His hair was mussed, his jacket open and his boots were leaving melting snow puddling on the floor. "Good, good," she murmured. "Thanks for checking for me."

She could see a muscle working, as if he were clenching and unclenching his jaw. And in a flash, she saw his father in him. That cold, hard front, that way D.R. had of staring at you, letting you twist in the wind while he waited to cut you off at the knees. "What's wrong?"

"You tell me," he murmured.

It was then she saw what he had in his hand—a manila folder and a plain brown box sitting to one side of the dresser, the top flaps open. Her box filled with information about Duncan and her folder with her notes in it had been in the trunk of her car. Everything she'd found out about him, everything she'd thought about doing to make the case successful. Figures. Dates. Her legs felt weak and she sank down onto the side of the bed. "How did you get that?" she breathed.

He came to tower over her, and she looked up at a grim man. He'd read everything. He knew everything. She didn't have to ask. It was written on his face. The man she'd made love with was gone. "The so-called accident was a setup?" he said, anger piercing his words.

"Let me explain. I never—"

He cut her off when he threw the folder onto the bed, the notes scattering over the mussed sheets. "It's all there," he said. "Your plan. Get to me, manipulate me. God, I regret ever setting eyes on you!"

She looked down, but cringed when she saw the papers scattered on the bed. She knew what was there. *Bishop is into control, needs to feel as if he's the one calling the shots. A rescue complex. Set up a scenario to make him the hero.* She knew every word and felt sickness rise in her throat. She had outlined her idea for the meet on the side of the road and she'd set out the financial deal with D.R. But not the most important things. Not the things she'd found when she really met him. She looked down at her clenched hands in her lap. "No, it's not all there," she managed to say.

"God help me if there's more."

"Why did you do this?" she whispered. "You never should have—"

"A morality lesson from you? Forget it. Rollie saw the box in the trunk, spotted my name on it in big letters and showed it to me. He didn't understand why my box would be in your trunk. He still doesn't, but I do."

She bit her lip hard, willing herself not to cry. She was not going to be some sobbing woman begging for forgiveness. She'd been doing her job and looking for a way to help, not hurt. But she'd ended up destroying everything. "I told you I was going to explain things, and you said it could wait. You said that you didn't care about my past or what was going on."

He hunkered down in front of her, the way he had at the cabin, but she didn't look at him. She stared hard at her hands. "We're going to play a game, you and me," he said. "And you'll answer me truthfully, yes or no. It's simple."

She shook her head sharply. "This isn't a game."

"Yes or no, Lauren. Yes or no."

She closed her eyes tightly.

She heard him exhale, then ask, "You met my father?"

"Duncan, I can't—"

"Yes or no," he said sharply. "One word answers, so you'll be less likely to lie. Did you meet my father?"

"Yes," she said in a low voice.

"He hired you?"

"I work for Sutton—"

"Did D. R. Bishop offer you money?" he demanded in a rough voice.

"Yes."

"Is he paying for you to find me, and get me to go back to the business?"

She swallowed sickness in the back of her throat.

"Yes or no?"

She couldn't move. She couldn't talk.

Finally, he touched her, cupping her chin with one hand, but there was no gentleness in it, just contained fury that tightened his hold on her to hover just this side of real discomfort. "Yes or no?" he demanded in a voice edged with hoarseness.

She jerked back from his touch, twisting to get away from him. She stumbled to her left, catching at the nightstand and getting to her feet. She was ready to leave, but she ended up caught in the corner formed where the bed met the nightstand. And Duncan was right there, standing between her and any escape. "Yes or no?"

"Okay, okay," she said, hugging her arms tightly around herself as she looked up at him. She didn't care that she was crying. She didn't care about anything except stopping this horror. "You're right. He bought and paid for me. Is that what you want to hear? He wants you back. He's willing to do anything it takes to get you back. He told me to do anything I could think of to make it happen, and if I do it, he's going to pay me a bonus."

"Was seducing me part of what he asked you to do?"

"He suggested it," she said, lifting her chin a bit, getting no satisfaction when she saw him flinch at her words. Then she added, "And I rejected it."

He shook his head, his laughter more disbelieving than in any way happy. "Damn you, you rejected it? What do you call what happened last night? And don't you dare tell me that it was real, or—" He bit off his own words, then uttered a profanity that rocked Lauren before he said, "This is done. I'm out of here."

When he turned, she reached for him, grabbing the arm of his jacket, and he stopped. He turned, looked at her hand on him, then pulled hard to free himself. "Go back to D.R. and tell him you blew it, that I'm gone and as far as I'm concerned, you're both dead to me."

"That's it?" She was in so much pain that anger was a welcome emotion. "You make your declarations, and to hell with anything else?"

"You've got it," he said.

"I can't explain? I can tell you why I—"

"I know why you did it." He pointed to the scattered

papers on the bed. "D.R. made you an offer you couldn't refuse. Now, I'm leaving. I'm out of here."

She went closer to him, but pushed her hands behind her back. She couldn't touch him. "You don't have to leave. I won't tell D.R. where you are or what you're doing. I promise. He won't ever know about Silver Creek or Rusty's Diner, or anything about you here. And I know something that—"

His eyes narrowed, as if he didn't want to look right at her. "That's funny. You making me another promise. As if I'd trust anything you have to say now."

Chapter Fifteen

"Wait, I promise you, I won't tell him anything," Lauren said.

He laughed, an ugly sound in the small room, a sound that made her flinch. "Oh, I finally get it. If I give you more money than D.R. offered, you'll keep all of this to yourself?"

"No, I don't want—"

"Or maybe you'd tell him I'm somewhere else, like, maybe Fiji, on a remote beach? Or maybe you can just tell the old man that I'm dead. That should do it, don't you think? If there's enough money, I just won't exist."

"Duncan, I don't want your money."

"You sure as hell aren't going to get any money on this deal. Sutton's done a lot of work for D.R., but this takes the prize."

"Sutton doesn't—"

"Sutton has dug up dirt on everyone who walked through D.R.'s door, and he always instructed the investigators to do anything necessary to get what he wanted."

His father's words, do whatever it takes. "He said that, but I never—"

"I'll hand this to you, you're damn good at what you do. You had me agreeing to something I hadn't even considered until you showed up—to go back." He shrugged and his eyes looked bleak now. "You listened as if you cared, and in bed—" He cut off his own words now with a sharp shake of his head. "Damn you," he breathed.

He'd never said anything about love during the night, and she was thankful she'd never said those words to him. Now she knew, as soon as he walked out the door, she'd been nothing to him. No, maybe that had happened when he found the box. "I'm sorry," she said as he turned to the door. "But I found out…"

He turned from her, jerking the door open, and leaving. The minute the door shut behind him, she moved toward it. She pulled it open and hurried out after him, running down the stairs, then crossing the empty second-floor hallway to the stairs to the lobby. But she got no farther than the top step when she heard Annie's voice.

"Good morning. Lovely day. What can I do for you?"

Duncan's voice came up to her, clear as a bell. "I'm checking out."

"Is everything all right?" Annie asked.

"Sure, just take care of the bill."

Lauren didn't listen any further. She went back to her room, and when she closed the door, the small space seemed horribly claustrophobic. She could swear Duncan's scent still lingered in the air. But he was gone. She couldn't stop him, even if she caught up with him. But she would keep her promise. D.R. would never know anything about Duncan from her.

She crossed to the bed, and with one glance at the papers scattered across the linen, Lauren knew everything that had gone wrong was because of her. She read her own writing, *has to come back willingly.* She'd underlined *willingly* in red. *Or it's all or nothing.* The amount of the bonus D.R. had offered was beside the words, circled in red.

She hugged her arms around herself again, tears falling unheeded as she sank down onto the bed. Whatever had been was gone. Whatever could have been would never be. There was only one thing left to do. She got up and started packing.

Three days later, Los Angeles:

DUNCAN NEVER THOUGHT he'd walk back into the Bishop building again, but there he was, going through the door, being greeted by startled workers who quickly put smiles on their faces. "Good afternoon, Mr. Bishop," Willie, the usual guard who stood by the door, called out to him.

"Nice day, Mr. Bishop," Rhonda, who manned the front desk, said with a forced smile.

He walked quickly past them all, knowing that they weren't just shocked by him showing up after six months, but by his appearance. He hadn't bothered to dress for the occasion. He was in his jeans, a blue T-shirt and boots, his jacket left in the rental car when he landed in a city bathed in eighty-degree heat. He headed for the private elevator to D.R.'s offices, hit the code and got in when the doors opened.

For two days he'd done nothing but sit in the cabin, trying to rid himself of the bitterness of Lauren's betrayal and his own stupidity. He'd come close, so very close, to falling into her plan. He'd come even closer to loving her. Now he got sick just thinking about her. He blocked his last image of her standing by the bed, still mussed from their lovemaking, her face pale, her lavender eyes wide, the lies coming out of her mouth.

The elevator stopped and he stepped out. Helen was at her desk, guarding the entrance, and when she saw him, her jaw literally dropped. He nodded to her. "Is he in?" he asked.

She nodded, then cringed when the old man's voice came out of the partially opened door to his private office. "This is unacceptable," he said. "This isn't going to stand."

"He's busy," Helen said quickly, getting up from behind her desk and heading for the door. "I'll just close this and—"

Duncan stopped her by touching her arm when he heard another voice in the office, a lower voice, a controlled voice, a woman's voice. Lauren's voice. "I'm sorry, Mr. Bishop, but that's all I have on your son. There isn't any more."

He motioned Helen to go back to her desk and leave the door ajar. The sound of Lauren just a room away made him want to turn and leave. But he couldn't, not when she went on speaking. "But I'm bringing you something else, something that you can use to do with as you wish."

The sound of her voice brought back all the anger and all the bitterness. It was as if no time had passed without her. Now he was listening to her make an offer to his father. What offer? He couldn't leave until he knew.

"No, you listen to me, Ms. Carter, and realize that I mean this. I know you found my son. I know you found out about him, what he's doing. Now you're telling me that—"

She cut him off, something few people ever attempted with D.R., her voice louder now, but still even. "Your son is gone. I don't know where, but..." There was a rustling of paper. "Here, this is yours."

"How much?" D.R. asked bluntly.

"It's free. From me to you."

More papers rustling, silence, then D.R. uttered, "My God, how did you find this?"

"Some digging."

"How much?" he said again.

"I told you, it's yours. But Sutton—"

"I pay for performance," D.R. said. "I'll have a check cut. How much?"

She named a figure that was twice what he'd been going to pay to her before. "And make it out to the Moss Free Clinic."

"Whatever you want," D.R. said. "But tell me one thing?"

"I don't know where your son is."

"You've made that clear, but tell me this, is he going to come back?"

"No," she said softly. "He won't be back, and I think that going after him again would be a huge mistake. He deserves to be left alone, to find his own life. And now that you have the other information I found, I think you'll be fine, too."

"This isn't the same, but if you're sure Duncan won't—"

"Trust me, Duncan won't be back anytime soon."

Duncan moved then, pushing the door open and stepping into his father's office. The old man was standing behind the desk, shock on his face. Then he looked at Lauren. "Don't trust her. I'm here," he said.

She looked different in a simple business suit and low heels. Her brilliant hair made her skin look pale, and her eyes, that improbable shade of lavender, looked smudged. But despite everything, she stirred something deep inside him. "But pay her the money she worked for," he said and saw her flinch at his choice of words. Words that he knew right then he didn't mean.

She'd had her chance to hand him over to D.R., to just tell him where he was, and she hadn't done it. "No," she said.

"Damn straight I'll pay her," D.R. boomed, over the shock and obviously feeling the stirrings of victory. "Helen, get in here," he bellowed as he came around the desk.

Helen scurried in, looking at the three people. "Yes, sir?"

"Get down to the business office. I need two checks. One made out to the Moss Free Clinic, and the other made out to—"

"The same place," Lauren said.

D.R. shook his head. "Whatever she wants," he said,

and told Helen the amounts, then clamped a hand on Duncan's shoulder. "I knew she was wrong, that you would come back."

"Yes, she was wrong. I'm back," he said, meeting D.R.'s gaze directly. Then he said what he came to say. "But I'm only here to get something straight. I shouldn't have walked out and left you to run roughshod over everyone and everything. I should have fought you, gone to the board, put pressure on to stop you, and now it's too late. So I'm here to say this is yours, and you can keep it. Call me if you want, come visit if you want, but from now on, you're my father, not my business partner and not my boss."

D.R.'s eyes grew tense as Duncan spoke, then the old man said, "Well, that's a nice little speech, but you know, it seems I might not need you around here, after all, thanks to Ms. Carter."

Duncan looked back at Lauren who stood silently watching the two men. "Thanks to what?"

D.R. turned and reached for a stack of papers on the desk, thrusting them at Duncan. After skimming the pages, Duncan looked at Lauren. "You found out about this David Kennedy?"

"That's what I wanted to tell you. I found out about your cousin, and I thought that he was your way out. It gave you a choice." She was clasping her hands tightly in front of her. "I just thought it would make up for things. But I was wrong."

He moved away from D.R., crossing to Lauren. She'd said she wanted to talk, to explain, and he'd thought it was all lies, just a ploy to keep him off bal-

ance until she could manipulate him into coming back
here so she could get the money. But maybe he'd been
wrong. Facing his father had been easy compared to facing Lauren now. "You knew about this before—"

"I thought I was on to something, then, just before
you came back, Madge called to tell me she'd tracked
down your cousin. It was the answer. I mean, I thought
it was. You wouldn't have to come back, and your father would have a Bishop to take over from him."

"What in the hell is going on?" D.R. demanded.

Duncan ignored his father. It was his life, right here,
right now, hanging in the balance. "What's the Moss
Clinic all about?"

"It's my brother Tim's clinic. They really need equip-
ment and funding. Since your father wants to part with
his money, I thought I'd put it to good use."

"Why don't you keep it? That's what you were after."

"At first, but now… I don't want it. I'm a pretty good
waitress, and I forgot how good the tips can be. I'll
make it."

"Oh, I get it," D.R. said. "You're not taking my money,
because you think you've got the big fish hooked."

Lauren paled at his words. "No, I don't have the big
fish hooked. I never did." She reached for her purse,
clutched it to her middle, then looked back at Duncan.
"Good luck," she said softly, then hurried around him
and out of the office.

He couldn't let her go and started after her, as D.R.
called, "Go ahead, I don't need you."

He didn't pay any attention, hurrying through the
outer office, into the hallway, to the elevators, where he

saw Lauren. He jogged to catch up with her, caught her by the arm and turned her around to face him. "You promised we could talk. I want to talk."

"Why?" she asked, and he felt her take a shuddering breath.

"I have to ask you a question."

"Please, don't start with questions. I'm sorry for everything. Isn't that enough?"

"No," he breathed, and looked around. "Come with me."

She didn't fight him when he lead her back down the hallway, past his father's office to what was once his own. Once inside, he shut the door.

"One question?" he asked.

She exhaled unsteadily and closed her eyes. "What?"

He moved closer, touching her, framing her face with both his hands. "Why didn't you take the money?"

She bit her lip, then her eyes fluttered open. They were overly bright, but not filled with tears the way they'd been three days ago. "I didn't want it," she breathed.

"Why?"

She moved away from his touch, looking around the room as if she wanted to escape. "Because I couldn't," she said. "I couldn't, and I can't do this. I can't be here with you answering questions. I can't do this."

"I can't just walk away. I've done it once too often in my life. I can't do it this time."

She hugged herself. "Neither can I. I need to go."

She made a move toward the door and he stepped in front of her, stopping her. "I can't let you."

She looked up at him. "What do you want from me? An apology written in blood? I'm sorry. I'm really sorry. I am more sorry than you can imagine that everything got so twisted and out of control."

He knew she was going to leave but he wouldn't let her go without saying something he had wanted to say in the middle of the night when he'd been loving her. "Lauren, I'm the one who's sorry. I'm sorry that I held you and touched you and lay with you."

She gasped at his words and tears welled in her eyes. She shook her head, and he could see the rapid breathing, and the way her breasts pressed against the confines of the navy jacket. "Stop," she said, covering her ears with her hands. "Stop it."

He caught her hands with his and pulled them down. "Not until I say one more thing," he whispered hoarsely. "I'm sorry I never got to tell you that I love you."

She didn't say a thing. She just stared at him, tears rolling down her cheeks.

"I'm not doing this right," he said. "I've never done it before. Hell, I can get in front of a board of directors and say everything I need to say without a problem." He exhaled. "But telling you I love you, it's got to be the hardest thing in the world. Lauren Carter, please, rescue me? Save my life?"

She moved then, reaching out to touch his chest, then pressed her palm to his heart. He didn't move. He couldn't breathe. He just watched her look up at him, then come closer and say, "Then we're even?"

"Forever," he whispered.

"I love you, forever," she breathed and went into his

arms, hugging him tightly, as if her life depended on holding on to him.

He knew his depended on her. He kissed her quickly and fiercely, then pulled back and looked down at her. "Now what?"

She smiled up at him, the tears still damp on her cheeks, and he brushed at them with his forefinger. "I think we need to go to a place where we can be alone and really talk."

He kissed her again. "I know just the place."

Thanksgiving:

IT SNOWED IN SILVER CREEK for Thanksgiving and everyone talked about the roads being closed again. That the plows were overworked, and the skiing would be the best ever when the snow stopped. Lauren didn't care about any of that. All she cared about was the man in bed with her in the small cabin near the best lookout point outside of town.

It was evening, the light failing and the fire in the hearth blazing. She snuggled into Duncan's embrace, kissing his naked skin, touching him and knowing him, and certain that she could never love him more than she did at that moment. She thought he was asleep, but he surprised her by moving, his hand finding her breast. She gasped softly and he drew back. "I'm sorry," he said.

She caught his hand and brought it back to her breast, holding it there. "Oh, no, love is—"

"Never having to say you're sorry," he finished on a low chuckle.

"You've got it." Then she gasped again, but this time because he moved closer to her and she felt him against her.

"Talking is overrated," he said in a rough whisper, then rolled on top of her, his weight supported by his hands on either side of her shoulders. "And wasting time is a sin," he finished as he touched her, tested her, then filled her in one smooth stroke.

They came together with an urgency that hadn't been sated by spending the better part of the past twenty-four hours in bed. And Lauren knew that it never would be sated. She'd want him more and more, never less. She loved him, and when they climaxed together, she told him how much she loved him. And as she drifted in his arms, letting the feeling linger, he spoke to her, his lips by her ear, his words soft and just for her.

When she woke, Duncan wasn't in the bed. She sat up quickly, then saw him at the fireplace putting on more logs. He was naked, and when he stood to come back to the bed, the firelight played over his body. He slid under the sheets with her and she snuggled into his side.

"With this snow, I'm betting the roads are blocked for at least today and tomorrow," he said, his fingers tracing patterns on her bare shoulder.

"And tell me again, why is that bad?" she asked.

He laughed softly. "It's very good. Rusty's going to be going crazy, but besides that, it's very good for a honeymoon to be uninterrupted."

She shifted, turning up on her elbow to look down at him and her left hand on his chest. The diamond he'd picked out at the gift shop near the chapel they'd gone to in Las Vegas glittered in the firelight. Married. They'd known each other only a short time, but when Duncan had asked her on the plane to marry him, it had felt very right to say yes.

"Should we tell D.R.?"

He shifted back in the bed, letting go of her hand to put his arm behind his head and stare at the fire. "Some day we will. After all, he is my father. But that's about it. Maybe he'll find the heir he wanted in Kennedy. Maybe not. But it's his choice, not mine."

She touched his face, making him look at her. "And how about you? Are you all right with that?"

"I'm fine," he said. "But we've got plans to make."

"I'm happy just staying here," she said.

"I am, too, but there's your schooling, and things to take care of."

"My schooling will be just fine. They have law schools around here, I'm sure. I'm done with being a P.I. I can work at Rusty's and, as I said, I make good money in tips, and I'll hit him up for a raise when I go back. You can, too."

He laughed then, a rich sound that thrilled her. "Oh, I guess we do need to talk." He covered her hand with his, pinning it to his chest over his heart. "When I came into town, Rusty needed help and I decided to invest in the diner. No strings attached. I did a few negotiations for him. So if you want a raise, it wouldn't hurt to be nice to me."

She laughed at that, ducking her head to kiss him, then drawing back. "Then we'll do okay," she said.

"You have a bit of the diner and I can make enough money to help with things."

He pulled her to him. "I guess I didn't make myself clear. I'm not broke. I had my own investments and money, totally separate from anything I did with D.R. In fact, I'm what some might call filthy rich."

She pulled free of him, sitting up, not caring that the sheets fell away. "Get out of here."

"Now, that I can't do," he said pulling her back to him, then rolling with her until he was over her, looking down. "Remember, love, you saved me. And I am not going to let you out of this deal for anything."

"I won't try to get out of it," she said. "Trust me."

He smiled that wonderful smile, showing the errant dimple. "I do. I do."

* * * * *

Look for more stories in
Mary Anne Wilson's new miniseries,
RETURN TO SILVER CREEK,
later in 2005.

The Rich Boy (#1065) is the fourth and final book in Leah Vale's popular series THE LOST MILLIONAIRES. The previous titles are *The Bad Boy, The Cowboy* and *The Marine*.

In this book, you'll read about Alexander McCoy. He's just found out that the mighty McCoy family, one of the richest in the nation, has a skeleton in its closet. When reporter Madeline Monroe discovers the secret, she will do anything she can to prove that she's more than just a pretty face. This is a story about two people from very different walks of life, who both want to be loved for *who* they are—not *what* they are.

I, Marcus Malcom McCoy, being of sound mind, yadda yadda yadda, do hereby acknowledge as my biological progeny the firstborn to Helen Metzger, Ann Branigan, Bonnie Larson and Nadine Anders et al., who were paid a million dollars each for their silence. Upon my death and subsequent reading of this addendum to my last will and testament, their children shall inherit equal portions of my estate and, excepting Helen's child, Alexander, who already has the

privilege, shall immediately take their rightful
places in the family and family business, whatever it may be at that time.
Marcus M. McCoy

Tuning out the chatter from the party going on the other
side of the study's locked doors, Alexander McCoy
slumped back in the big desk chair. Staring at the
scrawled signature at the bottom of the handwritten page,
he tugged loose his black tuxedo's traditional bow tie. If
only he could tune out the burn of betrayal as easily.

For what seemed to be the hundredth time, he had to
admit to himself that he was definitely looking at the
signature of the man he'd spent his life believing to be
his brother. The brother he'd initially admired, then set
out to be as different from as possible. And only Marcus would have had the nerve to belittle legalities by actually writing *yadda yadda yadda,* especially on something as important as an addendum to his last will and
testament.

Even if Alex could harbor any doubts, he would have
had a hard time dismissing the word of David Weidman.
The McCoys' longtime family lawyer had witnessed
Marcus writing the addendum—though David claimed
to have not read the document before sealing it in the
heavy cream envelope that bore his signature and
noting the existence of the unorthodox addendum in the
actual will.

A will that had been read nearly a month ago. Four
days after Marcus had been killed on June 8 while fly-
fishing in Alaska by a grizzly bear that hadn't appreci-

ated the competition. Before the reading of the will, Alex had grieved for the relationship he'd hoped to one day finally develop with his much older brother. Now…

Muriel Jensen's *His Family* (#1066) is the third book in her series THE ABBOTTS, about three brothers whose sister was kidnapped when she was fourteen months old. At the end of the second book, *His Wife,* we met China Grant, a woman who thought that she might have been that kidnapped daughter, but as it turns out, she's not. No one is happier about that than Campbell Abbott—who never believed she could be a relation.

Campbell Abbott put an arm around China Grant's shoulders and walked her away from the fairground's picnic table and into the trees. She was sobbing and he didn't know what to do. He wasn't good with women. Well, he was, but not when they were crying.

"I was so *sure!*" she said in a fractured voice.

He squeezed her shoulders. "I know. I'm sorry."

She sobbed, sniffed, then speculated. "I don't suppose DNA tests are ever wrong?"

"I'm certain that's possible," he replied, "but I'm also fairly certain they were particularly careful with this case. Everyone on Long Island is aware that the Abbott's little girl was kidnapped as a toddler. That you might be her returned after twenty-five years had everyone hoping the test would be positive."

"Except you." She'd said it without rancor, and that surprised him. In the month since she'd turned up at Shepherd's Knoll, looking for her family, he'd done his best to make things difficult for her. In the beginning he'd simply doubted her claims, certain any enterprising young woman could buy a toddler's blue corduroy rompers at a used-clothing store and claim she was an Abbott Mills heiress because she had an outfit similar to what the child was wearing when she'd been taken. As he'd told his elder brothers repeatedly, Abbott Mills had made thousands, possibly millions, of those corduroy rompers.

Campbell had wanted her to submit to a DNA test then and there. If she was Abigail, he was her full sibling, and therefore would be a match.

But Chloe, his mother, had been in Paris at the time, caring for a sick aunt, and Killian, his eldest brother, hadn't wanted to upset her further. He'd suggested they wait until Chloe returned home.

Sawyer, his second brother, had agreed. Accustomed to being outvoted by them most of his life, Campbell had accepted his fate when Killian further suggested that China stay on to help Campbell manage the Abbotts' estate until Chloe came home. Killian was CEO of Abbott Mills, and Sawyer headed the Abbott Mills Foundation.

Killian and Sawyer were the products of their father's first marriage to a Texas oil heiress. Campbell and the missing Abigail were born to his second wife, Chloe, a former designer for Abbott Mills.

When Chloe had come back from Paris two weeks ago, the test had been taken immediately. The results had been couriered to the house that afternoon. China had been there alone while everyone else had been preparing for the hospital fund-raiser that had just taken place this afternoon and evening. She'd brought the sealed envelope with her and opened it just moments ago, when the family had been all together at the picnic table.

They'd all expected a very different result.

After spending most of her life as either an army brat or a military wife, Bonnie Gardner knows about men in uniform, and knows their wives, their girlfriends and their mothers. She's been all of them! In her latest book, *The Sergeant's Baby* (#1067), Air Force Technical Sergeant Danny Murphey is in for a big surprise—Allison Raneea Carter is pregnant. With more than a little past history together, Danny has to wonder—is the woman who refused to marry him because she wanted her independence carrying his child? Find out what it's going to take for her to change her mind about marrying him *this* time!

Danny Murphey lay quietly in bed in the darkened hotel room and listened to the soft, rhythmic breathing of the woman beside him. He reached over and caressed the velvety smooth, olive skin of her cheek and was rewarded with a sleepy smile and a soft moan of pleasure. It was music to him after two endless years apart.

He found it hard to believe, after so much time, but Allison Raneea Carter was really here, lying beside him, in this bed. She had responded to him—they had responded to each other as if they were designed to be the other's perfect match. It seemed almost as if the past two years had never happened.

Technical Sergeant Daniel Murphey had dedicated that time to emptying out the dating pools of Hurlburt Field, Eglin Air Force Base, Fort Walton Beach and Okaloosa County, and had been ready to start working on the rest of northern Florida, when Allison had suddenly reappeared in his life.

He might have told his buddies back on Silver Team of Hurlburt Field's elite special operations combat control squadron that he liked playing the field, but he knew better. He had been trying to forget. Now that he and Allison had reconnected, Danny was ready to chuck it all and do the church and the little red-brick-house-and-white-picket-fence thing.

He'd been certain that he was ready to settle down two years ago, but Allison hadn't been. She'd wanted a career, and he, as a special ops combat control operator, could not envision his wife working. Men were supposed to provide for their families, and their wives were supposed to care for the home and their children. What better way to demonstrate his love than by wanting to provide for the woman he loved.

Allison hadn't seen it that way then, and it had caused a rift they had been unable to close.

They had never been able to compromise, and that one thing, for Allison, had been a deal breaker. She'd walked out on him, accepted a transfer and a promotion, and had not looked back.

Danny was sure that now, after two years apart, two years where he'd sown all the wild oats he'd wanted to and gained the reputation of ladies' man extraordinaire among the other members of his squadron, he and Allison would be able to compromise. He was okay with her working until the kids came along, and maybe when the kids were older and in school, she could go back. What woman wouldn't agree to that?

Allison shifted positions, giving Danny a tantalizing view of her ripe, full breasts. He could imagine his child, his son, suckling at her breasts, and the thought made his heart swell, as well as another part of his anatomy. He brushed a strand of her long, jet-black hair away from her face so he could gaze at her beauty. God, he could watch her all night and never be bored.

He'd always known that Allison was *the one*. And this time, he was certain that she knew it, too.

As much as he wanted to wake her, to get down on bended knees right now to propose, he'd wait. He wanted everything to be perfect.

He'd ask her first thing in the morning.

This time he was going to do it right. And this time he was certain she'd say yes. "Allison Carter, I want you so much," Danny whispered into the darkness. "I know you're gonna give in and let me take care of you."

He leaned over and dropped a light kiss on her soft, full lips, then he lay back against the pillows and drifted off into contented sleep to dream of what would be.

But, when he woke up…he was alone.

With *Hometown Honey* (#1068), Kara Lennox launches a new three-book series called BLOND JUSTICE about three women who were duped by the same con man and vow to get even. But many things can get in the way of a woman's revenge, and for Cindy Lefler, it's a gorgeous sheriff's deputy named Luke Rheems—a man who's more than willing to help her get back on her feet again. Watch for the other books in the series, *Downtown Debutante* (coming September 2005) and *Out of Town Bride* (December 2005). We know you're going to love these fast-paced, humorous stories!

"Only twelve thousand biscuits left to bake," Cindy Lefler said cheerfully as she popped a baking sheet into the industrial oven at the Miracle Café. Though she loved the smell of fresh-baked biscuits, she had grown weary of the actual baking. One time, she'd tried to figure out how many biscuits she'd baked in her twenty-eight years. It had numbered well into the millions.

"I wish you'd stop counting them down," grumbled Tonya Dewhurst, who was folding silverware into paper napkins. She was the café's newest waitress, but Cindy had grown to depend on her very quickly. "You're the only one who's happy you're leaving."

"I'll come back to visit."

"You'll be too busy being Mrs. Dex Shalimar, lady of leisure," Tonya said dreamily. "You sure know how to pick husbands." Then she straightened. "Oh, gosh, I didn't mean that the way it sounded."

Cindy patted Tonya's shoulder. "It's okay, I know what you mean."

She still felt a pang over losing Jim, which was only natural, she told herself. The disagreement between her husband's truck and a freight train had happened only a year ago. But she *had* picked a good one when she'd married him. And she'd gotten just plain lucky finding Dex.

"It's almost six," Cindy said. "Would you unlock the front door and turn on the Open sign, please?" A couple of the other waitresses, Iris and Kate, had arrived and were going through their morning routines. Iris had worked at the café for more than twenty years, Kate almost as long.

Tonya smiled. "Sure. Um, Cindy, do you have a buyer for the café yet?"

"Dex says he has some serious nibbles."

"I just hope the new owner will let me bring Micton to work with me."

Cindy cringed every time she heard that name. Tonya had thought it was so cute, naming her baby with a combination of hers and her husband's names—Mick and Tonya. Micton. Yikes! It was the type of backwoods logic that made Cindy want to leave Cottonwood.

Customers were actually waiting in line when Tonya

opened the door—farmers and ranchers, mostly, in jeans and overalls, Stetsons and gimme hats, here to get a hearty breakfast and exchange gossip. Cindy went to work on the Daily Specials chalkboard that was suspended high above the cash register.

"'Morning, Ms. Cindy."

She very nearly fell off her stepladder. Still, she managed to very pleasantly say, "'Morning, Luke." The handsome sheriff's deputy always unnerved her. He showed up at 6:10, like clockwork, five days a week, and ordered the same thing—one biscuit with honey and black coffee. But every single time she saw him sitting there at the counter, that knowing grin on his face, she felt a flutter of surprise.

Kate rushed over from clearing a table to pour Luke his coffee and take his order. The woman was in her sixties at least, but Cindy could swear Kate blushed as she served Luke. He just had that effect on women, herself included. Even now, when she was engaged—hell, even when she'd been *married* to a man she'd loved fiercely—just looking at Luke made her pulse quicken and her face warm.

HARLEQUIN *Super*ROMANCE®

On sale May 2005

With Child by Janice Kay Johnson
(SR #1273)

All was right in Mindy Fenton's world when she went to bed one night. But before it was over everything had changed—and not for the better. She was awakened by Brendan Quinn with the news that her husband had been shot and killed. Now Mindy is alone and pregnant…and Quinn is the only one she can turn to.

On sale June 2005

Pregnant Protector by Anne Marie Duquette
(SR #1283)

Lara Nelson is a good cop, which is why she and her partner—a German shepherd named Sadie—are assigned to protect a fellow officer whose life is in danger. But as Lara and Nick Cantello attempt to discover who wants Nick dead, attraction gets the better of judgment, and in nine months there will be someone else to consider.

On sale July 2005

The Pregnancy Test by Susan Gable
(SR #1285)

Sloan Thompson has good reason to worry about his daughter once she enters her "rebellious" phase. And that's before she tells him she's pregnant. Then he discovers his own actions have consequences. This about-to-be grandfather is also going to be a father again.

Available wherever Harlequin books are sold.

If you enjoyed what you just read,
then we've got an offer you can't resist!

Take 2 bestselling
love stories FREE!
Plus get a FREE surprise gift!

Clip this page and mail it to Harlequin Reader Service®

IN U.S.A.	IN CANADA
3010 Walden Ave.	P.O. Box 609
P.O. Box 1867	Fort Erie, Ontario
Buffalo, N.Y. 14240-1867	L2A 5X3

YES! Please send me 2 free Harlequin American Romance® novels and my free surprise gift. After receiving them, if I don't wish to receive anymore, I can return the shipping statement marked cancel. If I don't cancel, I will receive 4 brand-new novels every month, before they're available in stores! In the U.S.A., bill me at the bargain price of $4.24 plus 25¢ shipping & handling per book and applicable sales tax, if any*. In Canada, bill me at the bargain price of $4.99 plus 25¢ shipping & handling per book and applicable taxes**. That's the complete price and a savings of at least 10% off the cover prices—what a great deal! I understand that accepting the 2 free books and gift places me under no obligation ever to buy any books. I can always return a shipment and cancel at any time. Even if I never buy another book from Harlequin, the 2 free books and gift are mine to keep forever.

154 HDN DZ7S
354 HDN DZ7T

Name	(PLEASE PRINT)	
Address	Apt.#	
City	State/Prov.	Zip/Postal Code

Not valid to current Harlequin American Romance® subscribers.

Want to try two free books from another series?
Call 1-800-873-8635 or visit www.morefreebooks.com.

* Terms and prices subject to change without notice. Sales tax applicable in N.Y.
** Canadian residents will be charged applicable provincial taxes and GST.
  All orders subject to approval. Offer limited to one per household.
  ® are registered trademarks owned and used by the trademark owner and or its licensee.

AMER04R   ©2004 Harlequin Enterprises Limited

e♦HARLEQUIN.com

The Ultimate Destination for Women's Fiction

For **FREE online reading,** visit
www.eHarlequin.com now and enjoy:

Online Reads
Read **Daily** and **Weekly** chapters from
our Internet-exclusive stories by your
favorite authors.

Interactive Novels
Cast your vote to help decide how these
stories unfold...then stay tuned!

Quick Reads
For shorter romantic reads, try our
collection of Poems, Toasts, & More!

Online Read Library
Miss one of our online reads?
Come here to catch up!

Reading Groups
Discuss, share and rave with other
community members!

For great reading online,
visit www.eHarlequin.com today!

INTONL04R

THE ABBOTTS

A Dynasty in the Making

A series by

Muriel Jensen

The Abbotts of Losthampton, Long Island, first settled in New York back in the days of the *Mayflower*.

Now they're a power family, owning one of the largest business conglomerates in the country.

But…appearances can be deceiving.

HIS FAMILY

May 2005

Campbell Abbott should have been thrilled when his little sister, abducted at the age of fourteen months, returns to the Abbott family home. Instead, he finds her…annoying. After a DNA test proves she isn't his long-lost sister, he suddenly realizes where his prickly attitude toward her comes from—and admits he'll do anything to ensure she stays in his family now.

Read about the Abbotts:

HIS BABY (May 2004)

HIS WIFE (August 2004)

HIS FAMILY (May 2005)

HIS WEDDING (September 2005)

Available wherever Harlequin books are sold.

A new miniseries from
Leah Vale

The McCoys of Dependable, Missouri, have built
an astounding fortune and national reputation of
trustworthiness for their chain of general retail stores
with the corporate motto, "Don't Trust It If It's Not
The Real McCoy." Only problem is, the lone son and
heir to the corporate dynasty has never been trustworthy
where the ladies are concerned.

After he's killed by a grizzly bear while fly-fishing in Alaska
and his will is read, the truth comes out: Marcus McCoy
loved 'em and left 'em wherever he went. And now he's
acknowledging the offspring of his illicit liaisons!

THE BAD BOY (July 2004)
THE COWBOY (September 2004)
THE MARINE (March 2005)
THE RICH BOY (May 2005)

The only way to do the right thing and quell any
scandal that would destroy the McCoy empire is to
bring these lost millionaires into the fold....

Available wherever Harlequin Books are sold.